Tawny Weber

A SEAL's Desire

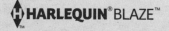

HARLEQUIN® BLAZE™

Recycling programs
for this product may
not exist in your area.

ISBN-13: 978-0-373-79900-8

A SEAL's Desire

Printed in U.S.A.

www.Harlequin.com

A *New York Times* and *USA TODAY* bestselling author of more than thirty books, **Tawny Weber** writes sassy, emotional romances with a dash of humor featuring hot alpha heroes. It's all about the sexy attitude! A fan of Johnny Depp, cupcakes and her very own hero husband, Tawny enjoys scrapbooking, gardening, spending time with her family and dogs, and hanging out with readers on Facebook.

Fans are invited to check out Tawny's books at her website, tawnyweber.com. For extra fun, join her Red Hot Readers Club for goodies like free reads, complete first chapters, recipes, insider story info and much more.

Books by Tawny Weber

Harlequin Blaze

Nice & Naughty
Midnight Special
Naughty Christmas Nights

Uniformly Hot!

A SEAL's Seduction
A SEAL's Surrender
A SEAL's Salvation
A SEAL's Kiss
A SEAL's Fantasy
Christmas with a SEAL
A SEAL's Secret
A SEAL's Pleasure
A SEAL's Temptation
A SEAL's Touch

Cosmopolitan Red-Hot Reads from Harlequin

Fearless

To get the inside scoop on Harlequin Blaze and its talented writers, be sure to check out BlazeAuthors.com.

All backlist available in ebook format.

Visit the Author Profile page at Harlequin.com for more titles.

To Birgit, for helping me find the heart of the story

1

"RIDE 'EM, COWBOY."

The cheer rang out across the sun-fried desert, making Petty Officer Christian Laramie grin as he blinded the second security camera perched high atop a rocky cliff.

Of course, his grin was only on the inside. On the outside, he was too busy rappelling down a hundred-foot vertical drop. With nary a crease or crevice in the sheer stone, he had to rely on the soles of his boots to control his descent.

He barely saw the laser flash in time to jerk to the left and kick into a spin. He circled too fast to see where the shot had come from, so could only judge by its trajectory. Close. *Too* close. Instead of wasting time trying to figure it out, or worse, having to dodge more fire, Laramie unhooked the D ring from his harness, tightened his grip and risked fast-roping the last twenty feet.

Not as easy as it would have been if nobody were shooting at him. Granted, the Multiple Integrated Laser Engagement Sensor gear meant the hits wouldn't be fatal. But that wasn't the point.

Because he was already free from his harness, the minute Laramie's boots hit the ground, he rolled for cover.

Crouched behind a large boulder, he jerked his shoulders to shed some of the sand. This was a communication-free maneuver, so he had no headset, couldn't ask his teammates for input. Instead, he listened carefully.

There. To the west, the sound of fabric on stone. Laramie angled his head around his boulder, assessing. Miles of hot sand were interspersed with rock formations, some tall, some wide. He watched the grouping to the west, eyes narrowed. Not on the rocks themselves, but on the sand to their left.

And booyah.

A shadow.

Grinning this time, Laramie kept to the rocks, skirting around behind the shadow's cluster and coming up behind.

He didn't need to see the man's face to know who he was up against. The man's size said it all. Laramie took a second to calculate how he was going to take down a man a good thirty pounds heavier and a hell of a lot more experienced than he was.

He had no doubt he could do it.

The calculations were simply to figure out how to do it fast, before he lost the element of surprise. He didn't have a clear shot from here, and if he moved he'd be spotted. So he went for the dive, low and fast to hit the man's knees. The element of surprise didn't last more than that, if the fist that swung around at his face was any indication.

The fight was down and dirty, each man struggling to hold the other and reach for their weapon. Laramie got a grip on his, pulled the SIG from the holster strapped to his thigh, but a swift chop to his hand sent it flying. He let it go, and using that brief moment of distraction, Laramie used an armbar manipulation to bring the other man's face to the ground, where he pinned him with a choke hold.

Knowing a captive was worth twice as many points

as a dead body, Laramie dug in his heels and, choke hold still in place, shifted to bring himself and his combatant to their feet. About halfway up, though, the guy made as if he'd lost his balance. The move pulled them both forward into a roll, with Laramie hitting the ground, back first. He was on his feet in time to watch the other man finish his own flight through the air, land with a thud, then twist to roll to his feet in a single smooth move that Laramie had to admire.

Until he saw the pistol in the guy's hand.

For a guy with the call sign Auntie, Castillo was one hell of a fighter.

Laramie grinned.

His eyes locked on the weapon, he anchored his hand to the rock, bending low and taking a deep breath as if the fight had left him winded.

He came up with a jump round kick, sending the gun flying. He feinted a palm heel strike to the face, wrapped his arm around the man's neck and took them both to the ground. Before they hit, he had the knife out of his boot and carefully pressed the dull side to the man's neck, tapping the sensor on his laser-engagement device to sound the hit.

As he did, a loud beeping sounded, then an air horn blared loud and shocking in the gritty air.

"Calling the win."

"That means you're dead," Laramie said, as he reached out a hand to the body on the ground. "And you owe me a beer."

"Dude, what's with the backup blade?" Clasping Laramie's outstretched hand to lever himself to his feet, Castillo gave the dirt on his fatigues a quick slap, then threw his arm over Laramie's shoulder.

Now that the battle was won, they were teammates

again. The sixteen-man platoon had split into two, each side battling "to the death" to test some new equipment. Laramie, O'Brian and Eckhart had led their side against Castillo, Morelli and Thorne's team.

"Know your enemy. I figured your team would have some heavy hitters and I'd need everything I could bring to the game," Laramie explained with a shrug. "That, and I saw the sheath inside the new boots and figured I'd try it out."

"Nice."

The two men strode off the mock battlefield, collecting the bodies of the others as they went.

"You girls call that a battle?"

The challenge bellowed out from a husky man so short that even standing there on that boulder, half the men on the team were still taller than him.

"Can I help you with your critique?" As ranking officer on the team during this exercise, Castillo's offer was both militarily correct in tone, and a clear *screw you* in message. Just one of the things Laramie liked about the guy.

"Warrant Officer Murdock," the troll-like man snapped, his words as sharp as his salute. "Here to take over CQC training."

"You're scheduled to report for Close Quarter Combat training on Monday at o six hundred hours."

"I'm here now." His heavy brow furrowed over beady eyes, the man spread his glare over the entire group before aiming it at Castillo again. "Do you have an issue with that?"

"Now why would anyone have an issue with that?" Fingers hooked through his belt, Castillo rocked back on the heels of his combat boots and grinned. "We're trained to deal with ambushes."

"Trained, my ass." Murdock bent at the waist to stare

into Castillo's face. "You call that dancing around you were doing training?"

"You're welcome to join us," Thorne called out with a tilt of his head toward the field. "Show us how it's really done."

"You think I'm afraid of your big bad club?" Murdock's laugh dripped with enough insult that Laramie felt as if he should shake it off his boots. "What makes you think you're all so special?"

"We're SEALs," sixteen voices chanted together.

"*Whatever.* I'm here to teach you pansies how to really fight." His words sneered down the extensive combat training and battle experience that each and every man there had under his special-ops belt. "The kind of fighting that requires more than guns or knives hidden in your socks."

The sidelong looks of amusement slanted his way made Laramie smile. Hell, that move had won the battle. Like the others, he began unbuckling and shrugging out of the vest that held the various laser sensors for their mock battle. Being the *last man standing*, Laramie's laser-engagement sensors were the only ones not lit, indicating he hadn't taken any hits.

As if seeing that as a negative, Murdock pointed at the flashing lights.

"You bubble-blowing babies don't even play with live ammo? What's the matter with you? Lasers all you can handle?"

All that earned him was an eye roll since the SEALs were known to regularly train with live ammo. It was rare enough that they hauled out the MILES gear that a few of them had had to be briefed on how to use it. But the commander expected them to train with all available resources, and laser practice was considered a resource. Something

Murdock probably knew if the disappointment on his face at not getting a reaction was anything to go by.

Still, while the platoon continued to silently strip down, Murdock continued his insult-laden introduction.

"The more you sweat in training, the less you bleed in combat."

"At least he's got his clichés down," Scavenger muttered with a laugh as he joined them. The bag of MILES gear he dropped at his feet muffled his words, but from the glare on Murdock's face, the warrant officer had a good enough radar to know he was being mocked.

"So…" He took a slow look at them, his eyes shifting from man to man with a look of distaste that reminded Laramie fondly of boot camp. "Let's see if one of you sissies can handle this new move. Any of you got the balls to step up here and take me on?"

That got him a slew of laughter and a few pats between the legs as some of the team checked their personal equipment.

"How about you, Anchor Clanker?" Murdock gestured to Laramie, using the derogatory reference to the anchors on the petty officer insignia visible on the collar of Laramie's camouflage jacket. "You think you can take me on?"

This time the laughter was aimed at Murdock. The guy was forty if he was a day, and those eleven years he had on Laramie weren't any kind of advantage in a physical contest. The guy might have skills when it came to close combat fighting, but they weren't likely to pay off in this situation.

Because Laramie was good. Maybe not competition form, but he held a second-degree black belt in jujitsu, he was fast on his feet and he had big hands. Big enough that it usually only took one punch to put a guy down.

Still, it was never smart to underestimate an enemy.

Laramie rocked back on his heels, assessing. The guy was older, smaller, but too cocky not to have some tricks up his sleeve. He was also fresh, whereas Laramie was coming off three hours of intense maneuvers.

So the minute the guy jumped down from his rock, knees bent and fists high, Laramie did a jump scissor kick, knocking him sideways. As soon as Murdock regained his balance and swung, Laramie blocked the punch with his forearm, launched a spring hip throw, then pinned him with a double arm lock.

And grinned down at Murdock's furious expression.

"Point?" he asked, wanting his pin acknowledged before he let the guy up.

When Murdock shoved, Laramie waited a moment just to make sure the guy knew he was *letting* him up, then pushed to his feet.

As he did, Murdock kicked Laramie's feet out from under him, sending him ass-down on the hard sandy ground.

"How's that for a point?" Murdock spat, lumbering to his own feet and slapping at the sand covering his uniform. "You didn't give me a chance to show the move."

"That," Laramie said bouncing back to his feet, his easy tone a vivid contrast to the other man's breathless one, "is how we do it."

"You mean by cheating?"

"If we ain't cheatin', we ain't trying," Laramie paraphrased. It was known among the SEALs that the larger force set the rules, and the team was always the smaller force. Therefore, to win, they broke those rules. "Bottom line, I won."

Which shouldn't be a surprise.

Because Laramie was a SEAL.

He made it a point to always win.

FOUR HOURS, A SHOWER and a hot oil massage from a talented blonde named Hilda, and Laramie was back in fighting condition. He strode into Olive Oyl's bar, his Stetson taking the place of his battle helmet, jeans instead of combat gear and his cowboy boots knife-free.

The Navy hangout located a few miles away from the base in Coronado, California, was loud. Music and laughter rolled over the top of the conversations, hitting Laramie in an inviting wave as he stepped through the double doors. Bodies were packed from one end of the long building to the other, proving why the bar's proprietor hadn't wasted a lot of time prettying up the decor. It was a man's bar. A sailor's bar.

The grayed wood floors were nicked, the whitewashed walls punctuated here and there with anchors, rustic ship wheels and a faded nautical compass painted over the bar itself. Neon bounced off rope-trimmed stools and the roving waitstaff wore wide-legged white pants, striped cotton nautical shirts and classic sailor caps.

Olive Oyl's was the go-to place for the SEAL teams. It was also the embodiment of all of Laramie's childhood visions of the seafaring world. He grinned. And a damned welcoming place.

He moved easily though the crowd, his rolling gait as much from spending his formative years on the back of a horse as spending many of his adult years on the deck of a ship.

He returned greetings and waves with ease, but didn't slow on his way toward the back rooms where the team usually met. At least, not until one particular greeting.

"Laramie!"

The breathy greeting was accented by a loud giggle and a bouncy little wave to get his attention. Laramie chuckled, appreciating what the bouncing did for the tiny strips of bright blue fabric masquerading as the blonde's dress.

Okay, he thought as he changed his heading, sauntering toward the woman. So he'd had a lot of sailor visions as a kid, but he'd bet the sexy side of those visions, the ones with naked mermaids and nubile port warmers, hadn't hit until he was at least thirteen. Maybe twelve.

As he approached the blonde, it only took a couple of flips through the little black book he kept in his mind to come up with a name. Terri, who worked as a cocktail waitress but wanted to be a movie star. She liked her chardonnay with ice, preferred Froot Loops for breakfast and had a penchant for doing it doggy-style.

"Hey, sweetheart," he greeted with a warm smile as he leaned in to prop one hand on the bar behind her. "How've you been?"

"Lonely." She batted her heavily lined brown eyes, the slight bloodshot hue cluing him in to the fact that she wasn't on her first drink of the night. "I've missed you."

"Is that a fact?"

Before he could even begin the mental debate over whether he was going to help her get over missing him tonight or not, another slender hand smoothed up his back, then tickled its way down.

He glanced to the right to see the sultry brunette, her short cap of hair and the little mole above her lip immediately clicking open the file. Stella, flight attendant with a penchant for leather, beer on tap and midnight sushi.

"Hey, sweetheart," he greeted, shifting his body so he was positioned directly and evenly between the two women.

"Hi, Laramie. I've been waiting for your phone call." She tiptoed her fingers up his back, wetting her bottom lip and sliding a dismissive look toward Terri.

Terri, however, wasn't easily dismissed.

"You'll just have to keep waiting," the blonde said, wrapping her arm through Laramie's and leaning in to his body so her breasts almost engulfed his arm. "He's with me right now."

"Why would he be with you when he has me?" Stella countered, her hand now tiptoeing down Laramie's front, as well.

Laramie tilted his head to one side, loosening the stiffness in his neck, then to the other. As the two women hissed at each other, he debated his options. Option one, pull them both close and suggest the three of them make a night of it. Option two, let them both down easy before either thought they had any rights to claim.

Even as his body suggested option two, because dammit, massage or not he was still sporting a corral full of bruises, he automatically slid into option one. Because, well, hey, two women and hot sex? Why not?

But just as he slid an arm around each slender woman, he heard a call.

"Ride 'em, Cowboy."

Laramie glanced down at the laughing comment, noting with amusement that three of his teammates were grinning at the show from their perch at the end of the bar.

"Need help?" another asked.

And just like that, the moment of peace between the two women exploded into a catfight. Laramie didn't know what set them off. Hell, he figured it wouldn't make sense to him even if he did know. The only thing he understood about women was how to pleasure one and how to walk away. Usually unscathed.

But as the blonde dived across his body, nails extended toward the brunette's face, he arched backward. Not in time to miss the brunette's response, which was a lousily aimed fist that missed the blonde and skimmed Laramie's chin.

"Okay, that's enough," he snapped with enough force to stop them both so that they stared, breasts heaving dangerously over the tops of their skimpy outfits and their eyes hot enough to fry rattlesnakes.

"Laramie—"

"But she—"

"Ladies." He angled a charming smile from one to the other, then despite the pain shuddering through his shoulder from the impact of the angry dive, wrapped his arms around the women again. He looked into brown eyes, then blue, keeping his expression easy and his tone as soothing as he would toward a skittish mare. "Two gorgeous women, both wanting my attention? I'm a lucky man. But as much as I would love to spend the evening with both of you, I'm due to meet my friends. So what d'ya say? How about we all kiss and say good-night for now. I'll catch up with both of you when I'm back in town."

It took a little more soothing, and more than a couple of kisses each, but Laramie was soon able to ease himself away. And, he noted as he made his way down the bar, he left the women happily chatting away.

"Impressive," intoned a Nordic giant most of the team called Ice. Ensign Dag Eckhart was six-five and built like one of the mountains from his homeland.

"Were you coming to save me?" Laramie asked with a grin, noting that the large man was on full alert, something he'd come to recognize from the way Ice's white-blond hair stood on end.

Ice was relatively new to the team, having only joined before their last mission. They'd just come off a two-month deployment that'd involved training foreign counterparts in strategic defense in a country that didn't believe in hamburgers, beer or fraternizing with women.

So he knew the man wasn't trying to be insulting. But the idea that there was any situation that involved the fairer sex that Laramie couldn't handle?

He'd thought his reputation was stronger than that.

Laramie tilted his Stetson back a little farther on his forehead and sighed.

Damn, he wanted a beer.

He didn't get two feet before he was surrounded by laughing teammates.

"Dude, why'd you stop them? They hadn't got to the hair-pulling and clothes-shredding part of the fight." Mick Samuels, aka Blackjack, looked as if he was going to cry in his beer. "You know that's the part I like best."

"You're a sad little man," Ice deemed, shaking his head in dismayed judgment.

"Everyone's little to you." Blackjack shrugged. "I'll bet you have plenty of dirty little thoughts, there, Dag."

Looking as offended as if Mick had just suggested his mama did dirty times with polar bears, Dag shifted his stance, looming over the smaller man.

Laramie just kept moving toward the room at the back of the bar reserved for the SEAL team. There, he lifted a finger to the roving waitress, then angled it toward Castillo's table. She responded with a wink and a look of interest that he debated while he took his seat.

"Looks like you might have plans for tonight," Castillo said by way of a greeting.

"Nah," Laramie decided. That didn't stop him from giving the leggy brunette a slow smile of thanks when she leaned close to bring him his order. He did a quick inventory, noting the bare ring finger, easy smile and hot appreciation in her eyes, then slid his hand over hers on the glass of beer. "I've got plans tonight."

The brunette looked disappointed, but slipped a folded napkin into his hand before sauntering away. He took a second to enjoy the swing of her hips, then tucked the paper into his pocket. He didn't have to glance at it. He knew it'd be her phone number.

"Nice of you to put Murdock on his ass," Castillo said. "Nothing like a little welcoming humiliation to cement his hard-on to outdo the SEALs."

"You're welcome." Laramie grinned, twisting the chair around to straddle it. "I'm only sorry I didn't put him on it a lot faster."

Castillo chuckled as he reached for his own beer.

"Guaranteed, that guy is gonna be a pain in our asses for the next four weeks."

"If you're lucky." At Castillo's questioning look, Laramie reminded him, "He reported for duty four days early. What d'ya wanna bet he'll try to extend training a week or three longer than scheduled?"

"Damn." Castillo's scowl only lasted a second before his grin busted it up. "We're due for predeployment as soon as Donovan and Thorne get back the first of the month. Murdock can stick around if he wants, but that's his expiration date."

"I ran into Murdock on my way off the island," Blackjack said, referring to the location of the Naval Amphibious Base Coronado, as he joined them. He knocked a chair back with one foot, then slid into it in one smooth move. "Crazy bastard was going on about how he was going to put us in our place. He's aiming hard for you, Cowboy."

"That's just fine. I'll be happy to kick his ass again when I get back," Laramie said in a slow drawl. "Guys like Murdock, they've always got things to prove."

"He keeps calling us girls, we might want to make it our business," Blackjack muttered into his beer.

Poor guy, he was still so green. Laramie shared a look with Castillo. They were gonna have to rub some of that shine off Samuels, PDQ.

"He keeps calling you girls, then as soon as I get back, we'll all just drop our drawers and crush his ego once and for all," Laramie told the new SEAL, downing the last of his beer as the others burst out laughing.

"My wife will vouch for mine," Castillo said with a smile. Laramie figured Genna would vouch for anything when it came to Castillo. Poor girl was crazy in love.

"What're your plans for the next three weeks?" Castillo asked, propping his size thirteen boots on the opposite chair. "You heading back to Texas?"

"First flight out."

"What d'you do there?" Blackjack grinned. "You working your way through a harem or two?"

As if.

"My plans for leave include three weeks of peace and quiet," he said, his words a little dreamy. "I'm heading for a small cabin in the Guadalupe Mountains. No traffic, no neighbors, not even a television."

"Seriously?"

At Laramie's nod, Blackjack's face fell like a three-year-old being told that Santa was a big fat myth.

"And the women?" Castillo asked, looking much less disappointed than the other man.

"I said peace. That means no women." Then, because his reputation demanded it, he added, "Most of these guys, they use leave to get all the women they can. Me? I get them all the time. I use leave to recoup."

"One of these days, Cowboy, you're going to find the right woman." Castillo's smile was wicked enough to assure Laramie that he wasn't offering a friendly assurance so much as wishing retribution. "And she's going to have you hog-tied and branded while you just sit there."

"I'm a tactical warfare specialist trained in recognizing, analyzing and neutralizing threats." Laramie shook his head. "In other words, that ain't never gonna happen."

No way in hell. He'd seen up close and personal what loving a man who put his career first did to a woman. And sure, some of the team might have found women who could deal with the pressures and demands—or so they thought. But Laramie was his old man's son. He had the same looks, the same thirst for adventure, the same kick-ass skills. It stood to reason he'd have the same talent for ruining the life of any woman crazy enough to love him.

"No way," Blackjack echoed, looking as offended as if Murdock had just come in and threw down pictures to prove the entire team was as dickless as he kept implying. "Cowboy is a legend. His reputation is unparalleled. Don't even jinx it."

"Don't worry." Laramie patted the guy's shoulder. "I'm completely committed to keeping the legend alive, buddy. Nothing's gonna jinx me. All things considered, I'm pretty sure I can avoid the trap."

"Yeah." Castillo gave a slow nod, his expression supportive. Then he tilted his glass in a salute. "I used to think that, too."

Laramie had heard about Castillo's rep. And Romeo's rep. And, damn, he stopped himself before he went through the mental list of SEALs who'd fallen to the marriage trap.

Nope. He shook his head.

"Believe me, I've armed myself too well to tie myself to one woman for the rest of my life. Me and marriage? Never going to happen."

2

"OH, LOOK AT YOU, Sammi Jo. Aren't you a vision of the perfect bride? A fairy princess about to start her happy ever after."

Was *that* what she was?

The Barclay Inn's elegant bedroom with its rose and gilt decor, the antique tester bed and rosewood cheval mirror were definitely fit for a princess.

But did that make her one?

Did the dress?

Her eyes narrowed at the mirror, Sammi Jo Wilson—Samuel Joseph on her oft-lamented birth certificate—tilted her head to one side and peered into the mirror. She tilted her head to the other side, trying to see if the dress actually had that kind of power.

Cream-colored, beaded lace hugged her torso from the strapless sweetheart neckline to the dropped waist. One side skimmed low on her hip, layers of organza flowing from the other side like flowers to form a petal that floated, layer after airy layer to the floor.

It was beautiful.

The most elegant thing Sammi had ever worn.

But its message was more along the lines of, *hey, scul-*

lery maid, go ahead and play princess for a day. See how that works out.

Sammi turned, the heavy fabric swishing as she twisted her neck to look at the back. Corset-styled cream satin laces crisscrossed down her spine to where the organza flowed again in another layer of petals.

Nope.

She wasn't getting the happy-ever-after vibe the wedding consultant kept talking about. But if they added a pair of luminescent wings and a wreath of flowers to her russet hair, she'd look like a fairy.

Her brow twitched.

Maybe that was the problem.

Fairy or princess, neither suited Sammi Jo Wilson of Jerrick, Texas. She felt like an imposter.

Maybe it was the whispers—most of them behind her back, but not all—wondering how on earth a girl from the trailer park had ended up engaged to the most eligible bachelor in town.

Maybe it was as Sterling had said when she'd confessed to him that she was having doubts; it was simply a case of bridal nerves.

Or maybe she was just an imposter.

No, no, no, Sammi assured herself. It was most likely that this wasn't her style. She was more suited to simple than elegant. To fun than fancy. To being in the background instead of standing under a spotlight on center stage.

She just had to convince the wedding coordinator of that. So, once again, Sammi took a deep breath and tried to find a compromise.

"Maybe this is a bit too much," she said as she maneuvered herself and her twenty pounds of dress back around to face the mirror. "I think I'd be better suited to a simpler dress."

"Oh, no. We won't be changing a thing." In an eye-searing-green pantsuit, Mrs. Ross fussed around Sammi. Her hands fluttered from the petal-like skirt to adjust the crafted silver bead rose on Sammi's hip, then flickered dangerously close to her breasts. "Mr. Barclay approved this dress. He also approved the Asiatic lilies for the bouquet and the string quartet for dancing."

A string quartet?

Sammi could only sigh.

"I was thinking it'd be sweet to use Sterling roses for the bouquet instead of lilies." At Mrs. Ross's blank look, Sammi added, "Sterling roses, for my fiancé, Sterling."

"Nonsense. The plans are approved. The wedding is in three weeks. This isn't the time to make sentimental changes."

"Oh, no. Can't muck up a wedding with silly things like sentiment," Sammi muttered on a sigh. The tiny rebellious voice in her head wanted to point out that it wasn't Mr. Barclay's wedding. Except that it was, her practical side argued. He was paying for everything, including the dress and jewelry.

And she was marrying his son.

So, really, it *was* his wedding.

Besides, Sammi owed Mr. Barclay so much.

And it wasn't as if she'd been dreaming of her wedding since she was a little girl. She'd never actually considered it a possibility until Sterling had mentioned that his father was hoping they'd marry. Next thing she knew, they'd set a date and Mr. Barclay had told Sammi she could use their nuptials as a test run for her suggestions that they host weddings here at the Barclay Inn.

"You do know how to dance properly, don't you?" Mrs. Ross asked with a doubtful look.

"I don't need lessons, if that's what you're suggesting."

Sammi started to shrug, but the dress was so heavy, she was afraid one good shoulder twitch and her breasts would flop out. Before she could ask if Mrs. Ross had changed anything else about the wedding, a whirlwind rushed into the room.

"Sorry I'm late. There was an accident on Old Marsh Road, ER was packed." Blythe Horton's words tumbled over each other much the same way her blond curls tumbled out of the bundled knot on top of her head. Her magenta hospital scrubs clashed with the lime-green frames of her glasses and, Sammi glanced down, her red plaid high-tops. "Whoa, Sammi Jo. Check you out."

"Pretty fancy, huh?" Sammi said, holding out both bare arms and twisting one way and then the other. She didn't do the full turn, figuring she'd had enough of a workout for one day.

"Fancy schmancy," Blythe returned with an eye roll. "You look like you should be getting married in El Paso or even Dallas or Houston. Not Jerrick."

"This dress is entirely appropriate for a wedding of the Barclay stature," Mrs. Ross interrupted with a harrumph, gesturing for Sammi to turn around.

Sammi sighed with relief. She could feel herself growing lighter as the older woman started unlacing and releasing her from the lacy confinement, so that when she stepped out of it to tug on her simple blue cotton robe, it was as if she were floating on air.

Oh yeah. She'd definitely be much more comfortable in something simpler.

"But isn't a wedding supposed to be about the bride?" Blythe kicked off her high-tops. "Not about the father of the groom's stature?"

"The groom is a Barclay, as well." Mrs. Ross unzipped the protective bag holding Blythe's bridesmaid dress with a metallic hiss. "Perhaps instead of criticizing things you know little about, you should practice telling time so as not to be late for any wedding-related events during the next three weeks."

"Sorry. All of those injured people distracted me from watching the clock," Blythe said with a sad shake of her head. She made a show of looking around the space, the elegant smaller bedroom as lovely as the rest of the Barclay house. "I guess the other bridesmaids were so punctual that they've been and gone."

"Nobody likes a smart aleck," the older woman snapped, her carefully drawn-on eyebrows arching almost to her modified beehive as she tried to stare Blythe down. But Blythe was an expert on disapproval. Sammi didn't even get to the mental count of three before Mrs. Ross gave up with a loud sniff and flounced out of the room.

"I love smart alecks," Sammi claimed as the door slammed. Grinning as Blythe laughed, Sammi found the shoe box marked with Blythe's name and set the heels on the floor next to the dress.

"That woman is a complete nightmare. Especially the way she lords over the dresses," Blythe muttered as she shucked her clothes with all the inhibition of a five-year-old. "Does she get paid extra to impose her views on everything? Has she demanded the cake be four tiers instead of three? Changed your jewelry again? I don't know why you put up with her."

"She's not a *complete* nightmare," Sammi defended halfheartedly. Mr. Barclay had carefully chosen the wedding coordinator, both for his only child's wedding and because he wanted an expert on hand to advise them before they launched Weddings at the Barclay Inn.

As both the bride and the assistant manager of the inn, Sammi was a little disappointed that he wasn't letting her handle it on her own. But it was the end result that mattered, she told herself as she unhooked and unzipped the amethyst satin dress on the hanger. In a few short weeks, she'd be married to a man she respected who'd then gain her the respect of others. And if this new venture worked as well as she hoped, she might even get that long-promised promotion to manager.

She gave a happy sigh. Manager of an inn that offered the loveliest wedding packages in western Texas. Didn't that sound awesome?

"Mrs. Ross knows this event will kick off Weddings at the Barclay Inn." She handed Blythe her bridesmaid dress, noting that it weighed a lot less than her own. "She's probably a little overenthusiastic."

"Uh-huh." Blythe twisted her mouth but didn't say anything else as she stepped into the dress. She tugged the fabric chest-high, then turned so Sammi could zip her up. Strapless and fitted to the hips like Sammi's, the rich purple exploded over the knees in petal-like layers. "I notice you didn't deny that she's lording over the dresses."

"The woman watched while I washed my hands to make sure I did it right before she'd let me touch my dress." Giving in to her own sense of the ridiculous, Sammi rolled her eyes.

"You manage the fanciest inn in the county, you're so organized it's scary and you have exquisite taste. Why wouldn't old man Barclay let you arrange your own wedding?" Blythe tweaked her shoulders this way, then that, arching her back and trying to make it look as if she had breasts holding up that fabric.

"I'm assistant manager," Sammi corrected meticulously. Don Reedy was the actual manager. Sure, he was away as often as he was here, given that he handled a number of

Mr. Barclay's properties. But he still had final say in everything, and the inn was run to his specifications.

"But didn't Barclay promise over a year ago that he'd promote you to manager?"

"Once I proved myself." Sammi nodded. And she had, hadn't she? In the past year, she'd increased reservations by 20 percent, arranged for the launch of a new website for the inn and had cut kitchen expenses by purchasing from local farmers and suppliers. "I think the wedding venture will do the trick."

"Hmm."

"You doubt me?"

"You, no." Blythe shook her head. "Barclay, yes. So far he's managed to give credit for everything you've accomplished to someone else. All the while, he's got you living on the property as a full-time caretaker while paying you minimum wage by claiming he's covering your wages with room and board."

Sammi waved that all aside with a flick of her hand. She'd explained plenty of times that while Mr. Barclay had *shared* the credit for those improvements she'd implemented, he'd still thanked her personally. And though it hadn't been her idea to take room and board instead of a salary, Mr. Barclay's reasons were sound. After all, any cash she made was like a red flag waving high over the town, just daring her mama to come sashaying in with her hand out. And Sammi did owe Mr. Barclay for paying for college, at least for the part that her scholarship hadn't covered.

Blythe unknotted her hair, letting it fall to her shoulders. As she fluffed it around her face, her eyes met Sammi's in the mirror.

"I suppose the RSVPs are coming in," she asked, her voice so casual it was an instant tip-off.

"They are and she's not," Sammi said, her voice as tight as the knot in her stomach. Buying time, she rummaged through a tackle box labeled Bridesmaids until she found a new comb to give Blythe.

"You're really going to get married without Cora Mae?"

"Well, I graduated high school without her. And college. Why should getting married be any different?" Sammi shoved her fingers into her hair, but they got stuck in the fancy French twist. Glad for the distraction, she started tugging hairpin after hairpin loose.

"Is she not coming because she objects to who you're marrying? Or because you don't want her there?"

Not want her there?

Sometimes it felt as if Sammi had spent her entire life wishing her mother would be there, really be there.

Like when she'd found herself home alone at ten when her mother took off for a week in Vegas with a guy named Spike.

Or at eleven when she'd been so excited to play an angel in the holiday show and had stood there on stage, waiting and watching the audience with her hopes high. Only to walk home alone with her tinsel wings drooping to find that Cora Mae had found herself a new beau when he'd stopped in at the Quickie Mart where she worked for cigarettes, and simply hadn't been able to tear herself away.

At thirteen, Sammi had given negative attention a try, getting into fights and ditching class. But after Cora Mae had skipped four meetings with the principal in a row, she'd had to accept that even that wouldn't work.

At sixteen, she'd told herself she didn't care anymore. She'd gotten a housekeeping job at the Barclay Inn and, with Mr. Barclay's help, she'd had herself declared emancipated. She'd left the trailer park, and her mother, behind. At least, that's what she'd told herself.

Except some sad part of her buried deep in her heart kept wishing otherwise. It was easy enough to ignore most of the time. It was just the occasional event, like Mother's Day, Christmas morning—or whenever that cheap beer commercial played on TV—that her heart ached a little.

But no amount of aching was going to change anything.

"Sammi?" Her hair fluffed around her face like static-charged fur, Blythe pointed the comb. "What's the deal? Why isn't Cora Mae coming?"

"Mr. Barclay put his foot down." Leaving her own hair still tangled with the couple of hairpins she hadn't found yet, Sammi hit the tackle box again, this time for a bottle of hair serum. She dabbed about a half-drop on the palm of one hand, then rubbed both together before smoothing them over Blythe's head. As her fingers slid through, separating the curls and taming the frizz, she met her oldest friend's gaze in the mirror. "He was right to ban her, wasn't he? I mean, she'd be a nightmare. You know how she is."

"She is a nightmare," Blythe agreed quietly, her eyes dark with sympathy. "She'd probably get drunk and dance on the tables, fall into the cake and hit on the minister."

It shouldn't be funny, but Sammi's lips still twitched at the image. She gave Blythe's hair a final smooth, then sighed and started searching for her hairpins again. Blythe found them faster.

"Still, it should be your choice," Blythe said, handing Sammi the comb.

But by not having to make the choice, she avoided the guilt of not wanting her mother at her wedding, dancing drunk on the tables with the minister. Was that so wrong?

"Why would anyone object to my marrying Sterling?" she asked instead of answering, focusing on Blythe's earlier comment.

"You are kidding, right?" Blythe snorted. "Bless her

heart, your mama probably figures that she has more reasons than a dog has fleas for hatin' on the idea of you marrying a Barclay."

Sammi didn't need to see Blythe's face to know that dislike for Sterling Barclay and the fact that grass grew green were about the only things she'd ever agree with Cora Mae about.

"That's ridiculous. Sterling is a great catch. Everyone says so. He's handsome and cultured. He's intelligent and well-read and ambitious." Sammi's stomach tightened as she searched for more and came up blank. Then she caught the look on her best friend's face.

"What?" Sammi's stomach tightened again.

"Just, well, there are rumors going around again. I'm not saying it's true or anything, but there's talk that Sterling has been seen with one of the waitresses at Longhorn's."

Sammi had to swallow hard to get past the knot in her throat. It wasn't as if she and Sterling were a love match, or even marrying for hot, wild passion. But that didn't mean he'd cheat on her, did it?

Her fingers clenched and unclenched as if she could grab the dots dancing in front of her eyes and squeeze them into oblivion, but after a couple of seconds, Sammi was back in control enough to see the expression on Blythe's face.

Her spine immediately stiffened.

Best friend or not, the last thing Sammi wanted was pity.

"Oh, that," she said with as airy a laugh as she could manage. "It's nothing."

"Sammi—"

"Did you want to look at the jewelry choices before the others get here?" Sammi interrupted. "I want you to have first pick."

As if they'd been waiting for their cue, the door sprung open and with it, three women bounced into the room. She welcomed them with a grateful smile. She'd deal with wondering about Sterling and the waitress later. Right now, she had friends to greet.

And greet, they did, with their usual laughter, hugs and exaggerated air kisses. She'd roomed with Amy and Mia when they were at the University of Texas in El Paso, and had met Clara when she'd come to visit her sister Mia. She'd always be grateful to them, not only for helping her adjust to college life but because, thanks to them, she'd managed to develop a sheen of sophistication. Granted, her sheen was only surface and theirs went skin-deep, but she'd take what she could get.

"Hey there, Blythe," they greeted, their tone a shade cooler. Given that Blythe was offering a stony stare, the chill wasn't surprising. Sammi didn't know if it was because they were out-of-towners, because they were country-club sleek or simply because they represented a different part of Sammi's life—one Blythe wasn't part of. But Blythe had taken an instant dislike to the other women.

"Sorry we're late," Amy said with a breathy laugh that went perfectly with her sultry looks. From her long mink hair to her this-season Louboutins, Amy screamed luxury.

"We'd have been on time if a certain *someone* hadn't been indulging in a little afternoon delight with her new hubby." As no-nonsense as her gamine-cut ebony hair and simple linen pantsuit, Clara shot her sister a chiding look.

"Whine, whine, whine." Mia said, dismissing the criticism with an airy wave of her hand, her glistening wedding ring catching the light, sending rainbow sparks around the room. "We're newlyweds. We're supposed to have uninhibited, spontaneous sex as often as possible. Right, Sammi?"

"I'm not a newlywed yet, but I'll be sure Sterling knows

that rule," Sammi joked, pushing her hand through her heavy fall of hair.

Now that it was combed out of its fancy twist, the russet waves tumbled wildly around her face, so she grabbed a clip to pull it back. As she did, she noticed three pairs of eyes lock on her left hand.

Her bare left hand.

As one, they frowned. Clara opened her mouth, then snapped it shut again when Mia stepped on her foot. All three started talking at once, so the room was filled with random observations about Blythe's dress, the weather and how many calories there might be in lemonade.

Sammi sighed. She'd rather ignore it, but she knew it was better to head off their concern.

"Did I mention that Sterling is having his mama's rings redone for me?" she said with a little laugh, curling her fingers into her lap. Granted, it was his mama's cocktail ring and they'd visited the jewelers for the fitting a month ago. But that was beside the point. "It's taking a little longer to get them back."

"Oh, there's nothing like an heirloom," Amy gushed, giving Sammi's shoulder a friendly rub.

"Oh, I have something for all of you," Sammi exclaimed as if she'd just remembered. She hurried over to the glossy writing desk where she'd left the envelopes. She'd actually planned to give them each the hand-painted cards as they were leaving. But hey, why pass up a good distraction?

"Oh, Sammi Jo," Mia breathed as she opened hers.

Still, Sammi bit her lip as they all sighed and murmured their delight, each woman, including Blythe, showing the others her card and exclaiming over theirs.

"I'm so glad you like them."

"Like? Oh, no, love." Amy traced her finger over the delicate watercolor roses twining around the elaborately lettered *Thank You* before giving Sammi a beaming smile. "You are so talented. You could make a living painting cards, Sammi Jo."

"You did for a little while, didn't you?" Mia asked, holding her card, with its long, leggy irises, close to her chest. "Or was that only in college?"

She'd had quite a small business going in college, painting cards, wall hangings and the occasional stationary set to supplement what she made waiting tables. Most semesters her art had not only covered the cost of books, it'd given her enough to actually fit in with her friends instead of standing out like a country bumpkin. But once she'd come home and started working at the inn, she'd been too busy for painting, except the occasional gift.

"I dabbled," Sammi said, shrugging as if she hadn't hated to give up that dream.

"You could still dabble," Blythe pointed out, carefully tucking her sunflower-covered *Thank You* back in its envelope.

"Maybe after you're married," Clara said. "I'll bet Sterling would love it if you spent more time on your art."

Sammi didn't think Sterling was even aware that she painted. Thankfully, Mrs. Ross chose that moment to barrel into the room, saving Sammi from having to comment. As she began leading the women through their fitting, the talk bounced more naturally now, the women sharing their latest gossip while Sammi curled up on the bed, her robe draped around her feet as she enjoyed the vicarious fun.

"Sammi, has Sterling finalized your honeymoon plans yet?" Amy asked as she preened at her reflection in the mirror.

So much for fun.

"Honeymoon?" Sammi bit her lip. She didn't want to tell them that Sterling had decided to put off the honeymoon for a couple of months until they were both less busy. So she went with, "Oh, no. He's keeping it a surprise."

"I so admire your patience, Sammi Jo." Mia stood with her arms wide as Mrs. Ross pinned and tucked her sapphire dress to a perfect fit. "I was all over Conner about the arrangements months before the wedding."

"You're always all over Conner," her sister muttered, earning a snicker from Blythe.

"How do you know what to shop for if you don't know where you're going?"

"Not everyone is a shopaholic, you know." Holding up one lipstick and then another to the mirror to check the color against her dress and her complexion, Clara paused to roll her eyes at Amy. "Some people actually wear the clothes they already have instead of shopping for an entire wardrobe."

"Says the woman with fifty lipsticks in her bag," Mia responded laughing.

"Amy is right, though," Clara declared as she tried on a pale pink lipstick, then wiped it right off. "Even if you dress from your wardrobe for the honeymoon, you'll need something extra sexy for your wedding night."

"Extra sexy?" Sammi repeated, frowning down at her robe-covered body. Under her practical cotton was more practical cotton. Why would she bother with anything else?

As if hearing her thoughts, the other women dove into a discussion on the merits of various lingerie styles when it came to the art of seduction. When the talk turned to sex play, Sammi had to force herself not to run, screaming, from the room. She pressed her hands against her churning stomach.

Just bridal nerves, she assured herself. It was natural to be nervous. Totally normal to freak out. She knew lots of women who'd been nauseous before their wedding day.

Granted, they were pregnant. She didn't think she could lay her nausea on that without the blessing of divine intervention.

After all, she and Sterling had never had sex.

Which wasn't a big deal.

She'd seen enough evidence in her life that sex was better left off the table. People either put too much meaning on it, so that it became an obsession that screwed up their lives. Or the only value they put on it was the mileage they got out of bragging about it after the deed was done.

The only lingerie that suited her attitude toward sex was a flannel nightie or, maybe, a chastity belt.

Not that she'd say that aloud. They were all friends—good friends—but she just couldn't talk about that sort of thing.

Except with Blythe. Sammi's gaze cut over to the bubbly blonde being tucked and pinned into her dress. Blythe was like a sister to her. They told each other everything. But she hadn't found a way to tell her best friend since first grade that she hadn't slept with the man she was about to marry.

She'd thought about pointing out that there was nothing wrong with saving yourself for marriage.

But Blythe knew perfectly well that Sammi had had sex before. So she was going to want specifics on why Sammi hadn't had it with the man she was about to commit the rest of her life to.

But Sammi couldn't explain that it just didn't matter to her. She wasn't marrying Sterling for sex. Nor, as so many whispered, was she marrying him for his money or his family connections. She and Sterling didn't need sex to make a good marriage. They had family ties, respect and common interests. They had a friendship, and that was way more important than sex.

The sound of her name amid naughty giggles pulled her from her reverie.

"I'm sorry, what?" she asked the group of wicked-eyed women staring at her. A group, she noted, that now included Blythe. Was there something about getting undressed together that made women best buddies?

"I asked if you prefer panties or thongs," Amy said with a naughty smile. "Then Mia asked if you had a preference when it came to fabric. You know, heavy silk or see-through lace."

How about cotton briefs and in the dark, with the lights off. Her face heating, Sammi cast a quick look around. Where the hell had Mrs. Ross gone? Why was the woman always around when she didn't want her and never here when she needed her?

But apparently sometime during Sammi's mental side trip through her nonexistent love life, the wedding coordinator had brought in a tray of delicate desserts and champagne.

And all of them, except Blythe, who'd tugged on her scrubs again, were sitting around in their undies, sipping champagne and nibbling bonbons.

"We're trying to figure out your lingerie style," Clara explained, actually pulling a leather-bound notebook from her messenger bag. "And are you going to want to branch out a little? Is Sterling into the kink?"

Sammi's mouth dropped.

But no words came out.

It wasn't their expectant looks that shocked her, so much as how perfectly normal they all seemed to feel asking such intimate questions. Not even in college had her underwear choices come into conversation. But now that she was marrying, everybody thought it was their business?

"Speaking of kink... Guess who's back in town?"

Taking pity on Sammi's horrified expression, Blythe addressed the question to everyone—and in a friendly tone, too. "This guy is amazing. Think orgasms by the dozen. The man every other man envies. Sergeant Satisfaction, Captain Climax, General G-Spot."

That's all it took to bring an image to Sammi's mind of a wicked smile, warm hazel eyes and toffee-colored hair with just a hint of curl. Even as a teen, the man had exuded sex appeal, so much that people rarely looked past it to see what a sweet guy he was.

To Sammi, he'd been a hero. He'd protected her from bullies when she was seven, then when he'd learned that they were harassing her because she couldn't read yet, he'd taught her in secret himself. He'd made Sammi feel as if she could do anything. His unquestioning belief in her had been a turning point in Sammi's life. Years later, he'd even helped Sammi get her job here at the inn. Talk about a hero.

"Laramie's back?" Sammi said a second before Amy did. Everyone giggled except Sammi, who was wondering why Amy would know Jerrick's bad boy. She'd grown up in Abilene, not Jerrick.

Blythe continued talking before Sammi could ask, and before she could analyze the tight feeling in her stomach over how Amy—or any woman under the age of thirty-five if the rumors were to be believed—would know Laramie.

"Long and lean, sexy as sin and hotter than Hades." Blythe made a show of fanning her hand in front of her face. "He's fueled the fantasies of every woman in town from the age of fifteen to fifty."

"He's fueled fantasies in a lot of towns, from what I hear," Mia chimed in. "Laramie is a legend in West Texas."

"I heard rumors about him when I was at college in San Antonio," Clara mused, looking modest in her simple silk teddy. "Didn't he go off to become a secret agent or something?"

"I heard he was a drug lord, although some people say he's really DEA and that's a cover."

"No, no," Amy interrupted. "He's a cowboy. He's riding broncs in the PRCA, you know, the rodeos. He was in Las Vegas last year for National Finals."

Actually, he'd left Texas to join the Navy twelve years ago. By now, he'd probably achieved his dream of being a SEAL. But Sammi kept that to herself.

"Guys like that are bad news," Clara declared, dabbing her lips with a napkin before she rose to dress. "Nothing more than man-whores."

"Laramie isn't bad news," Sammi defended, not able to let that comment go by. "He's really a sweet guy."

"Ooooh," echoed every voice in the room.

"Not like that." Sammi rolled her eyes. "I knew him when we were kids. He even got me the job here at the inn."

Actually, he'd found Sammi trying to hitch a ride to the bus station with grand plans to run away. He'd convinced her that running wasn't the answer over an ice cream sundae, then brought her to the inn where he'd convinced Mrs. Reed the housekeeper to hire her.

"That's right," Blythe remembered. "His mom worked here before she died."

"I'll second the sweet-guy vote. And it's unfair to call him a man-whore," Amy said. "I've never heard of Laramie costing women anything more than a little heartache."

"A little heartache is a fair price for the kind of memories he's credited for. I've heard he can go all night, rocking it like a jackhammer. And that smile." Blythe popped a grape into the air, caught it between her teeth, then bit into it with a snap and a grin. "Panty melting."

"Just what every woman wants. Melted panties." Sammi

frowned, wondering why everyone seemed to think sex was so damned important. Sex was messy and awkward, usually made up of mythical expectations and ridiculous requirements.

"You'll see," Mia said, giggling as she slipped into her Alexander Wang dress. "A few months of honeymoon sex, and I'll bet you melt every pair you own."

Since she didn't figure sex—not even sex with a legend such as Laramie—could be worth a single pair, Sammi could only laugh.

"Not to worry. You'll have enough panties to get you through a year of hot sex," Clara assured her with a comforting pat on the shoulder. "The lingerie shower will ensure that."

"A lingerie shower?" Sammi paused in the act of pulling on her jeans to frown. Her eyes shifted from one woman to the other. But they looked as surprised that she'd asked as she was to hear about it.

"You know, a shower for lingerie," Amy said, her expression two shades away from condescending. "Next Friday afternoon."

"I know what a lingerie shower is," Sammi said, trying not to clench her teeth. "I thought we were having a couple's bridal shower."

"I'm throwing the couple's shower," Clara said, looking up from repacking her cache of lipstick. "We're each giving you one. Amy, Mia and I."

"Three bridal showers?" *Three?* Her mind echoed faintly. But why?

She shot Blythe a desperate look, but her friend was nodding along as if having three separate showers was completely reasonable. That or she'd bonded with the other women over sex talk.

"I've got your bachelorette party covered," the traitor

said, tucking her feet back into her high-tops. "And don't worry. I'll make sure it's a party hot enough to melt your unmarried panties right off."

It was all Sammi could do not to cover her butt with her hands and tell them all to leave her panties alone.

3

"SAMMI JO, DID YOU hear who is back in town?" Fiona Green set down the last of the boxes of vegetables she was delivering to wave a hand in front of her face. "Hoo, baby, it's gonna be a hot couple of weeks."

"Because Laramie's back?" Sammi asked absently, paying more attention to the order she was checking than to the tenth announcement today of Laramie's return. All around her the kitchen hustled and bustled through breakfast service, the cacophony of voices, dishes and cooking soothing after a night of lousy sleep.

"Laramie. The man is drool worthy. He's the kind of guy who just looks at a woman and, poof," Fiona blew on her fingertips, "her clothes disappear."

"Uh-huh." Sammi Jo grinned as she signed off on the delivery. "Good luck staying dressed."

"You don't know what you're missing."

"You do?" Sammi's smile dimmed. Fiona had been a couple of grades behind her in school. How young did Laramie like them?

"No, but I know women who have. And they've told me."

"Ahh." Relieved, and late, Sammi said her goodbyes

and scurried around two waiters, the line chef and a bus-boy, double-timing it to the dining room.

What was it with everyone's obsession with sex?

She tried to wrap her mind around it all.

First the bridesmaids—and in the stuff of nightmares, Mrs. Ross. Then her newest guests had asked to change rooms three times, all in search of a bed that gave the best bounce. If that wasn't enough, her favorite sitcom had launched a new storyline about—yes, of course—sex.

Added to that, all the staff could talk about was the fact that Laramie was back in town. Two of the maids appeared to be wearing lingerie—while another had asked for the day off to go to the spa for a body buff and glow. Last night, even the kitchen staff had debated what foods were best to seduce the man.

Sammi Jo felt as if she should warn poor Laramie. Or she would if she wasn't so irritated with everyone putting all of the sex thoughts in her head—and a little afraid that with this theme, she'd see her mother sashaying through at any time in Daisy Dukes and pink pumps.

And then there were the cheating rumors. Those she'd rather ignore, but the sidelong glances and pitying looks she'd garnered over the past few days warned her that the issue couldn't be avoided.

Which meant she had to talk to Sterling.

Sammi glanced at the clock on the wall, winced and hurried through the staff entrance to the inn's dining room. The morning sun already shone bright through the wide, arched windows. It was gratifyingly full for a Thursday morning. The dining room boasted twenty tables clothed in white with matching china and pretty carafe center-pieces. The window's arch was echoed in the entry, where Sammi Jo had switched out the hostess stand for a ma-hogany piecrust table. The overall effect was elegantly cheerful, she thought as she moved through the tables, pausing to check with the head waiter to make sure nobody needed her help.

"Good morning," she greeted when she reached the table next to the window. "I'm sorry I'm late. We're a little short staffed in the kitchen."

"I was afraid I was going to have to eat alone," Sterling said with a wink as he set aside his iPad.

Sammi slid into her seat, smiling at her fiancé. Dark eyes contrasted with his wheat-blond hair, and while maybe his lips were a little thin and his chin a smidge weak, he had a clever personality and a Yale polish that made quite a package.

She was glad that he was so much more than a walking, talking erection with roaming hands and a one-track mind. Then her smiled dimmed. Maybe it was only with her that his mind never hit that track? They were to be married in three weeks. She knew he was interested in sex; there were too many rumors to pretend otherwise. But if she asked, what if she found out something she didn't want to know. Like, what if he was a closet deviant? What if, after they married, he'd want to wear her new underwear and have her spank him with chilled vegetables? Was that worse than him not wanting her at all?

In reality, she didn't want him. Not in that way, she admitted, twisting her fingers together in her lap.

"Sammi Jo? Is everything okay?"

No, she wanted to scream. She had no interest in sex, she didn't like sex and she thought life was much tidier without sex. Yet, the only thing she could think about now was sex.

Her lips trembled, but Sammi managed to hold back the crazed rush of babbling nerves.

"I'm sorry. I'm just distracted by work. Don has us short

staffed again, and we're having some tech issues at the front desk. Add in the wedding hoopla, and I'm a little frazzled." She swirled her hand in the air to emphasize her words, hoping he'd put her odd tone down to being overwhelmed. "I wish we could have something a little more low-key."

Something that didn't require Mrs. Ross, for instance.

"I know, I know." Sterling set his coffee down, dabbed his napkin to the corners of his mouth, then gave her the smile that made him such a good salesman. Earnest and charming, with just a hint of persuasive guile. "But Sammi, this wedding is about more than us. It's about the image we present to the community. Look at it as a networking opportunity. The guest list is impressive, the gifts will likely be cash and the entire event will make good press. That's good for our businesses."

Seriously? She was working double time to prepare the inn for its debut as a wedding destination, hearing honeymoon advice from the gardener and being nagged to death by Mrs. Ross over stupid details she didn't care about while being overridden on the ones she did. And all for the good of their businesses?

Stomach tight, Sammi wanted to lean across the table and tell him that she'd had enough. Sterling wasn't the one dealing with the wedding planner from hell. If he wanted to improve his damned business, he could take out an ad.

"You're right," she agreed, absently rubbing the knot in her shoulder. "I'm a little overwhelmed. Added to all of that are the new software changes your father wants implemented and the insane things my bridesmaids are saying. I suppose it's just been a rough couple of days."

Sterling reached out to lay his hand on hers again, this time giving it a quick squeeze.

"You worry too much, Sammi Jo. Let the wedding coordinator do her job and don't let your bridesmaids drive you crazy," he suggested, his smile a little less easy now. "As for the computer, I actually need to use it and your office this morning."

"I'm scheduled to do office work until noon. Your father expects me to have the new computer software installed and all the files transferred before the first of the month," she said before taking a sip of her sweet tea.

Sterling's smile slid away to be replaced with a dark scowl. Sammi sighed. All it took was the mention of Robert Barclay to put that look on Sterling's face. Oh, she knew Mr. Barclay could be difficult, but she was sure in time father and son would overcome their differences. It'd been her attempts to build that bridge when Sterling had moved back home last year that had brought her and Sterling together.

Someday, Sterling would appreciate his father for the great man that he was. As far as Sammi was concerned, Mr. Barclay had saved her life. It was thanks to Mr. Barclay that she'd gotten out of the trailer park and had made something of herself.

She owed him a lot.

The least she could do was try to help smooth things out between him and his only child.

But sometimes, the smoothing was a lesson in frustration.

"If you don't want me using your computer, just say so."

His words were stiff as he turned to greet the perky brunette waitress as she set a basket of minimuffins and pastries on the table. Darla refilled his coffee, asked Sammi if she wanted more tea and took their order before sashaying away again.

Sammi waited until she was out of earshot.

"I don't have a problem with you using the computer,"

she said quietly. "I can finish up my work this evening after my shift."

Sterling took a moment, but finally gave a brief nod.

"So what silly ideas are the ladies coming up with?" His tone was somewhere between placating and cheerful, but the expression on his face made it clear he wasn't happy. "Are they fussing about the dress choices?"

Sammi started to tell him about their silliness over Laramie, but found herself leaning closer instead and saying, "There are rumors that you're having an affair."

Again. The unspoken word hung in the air for a moment as Sterling blinked, then gave a deep sigh. He looked around as if to ensure nobody was listening, then reached over to pat her hand.

"First off, we're not married yet. Whatever we do between now and the wedding is our own business, isn't it? Besides, we've talked about this, Sammi. We're perfectly compatible in so many other ways. Just not that one. Why is this an issue?"

How did he know they weren't compatible sexually if they'd never had sex? Sammi pressed her lips together to keep from asking. Because he was right. Theirs wasn't a love match. They were friends—good friends—with respect and affection for each other. They'd agreed that their marriage was going to be more of a partnership than anything else.

Still…

"We've also talked about how essential respect and consideration for each other is, and why it's important to both of us to do our best to keep up appearances. We'd agreed that for all intents and purposes, we would give the impression of a love match." Despite the nerves clenching tight in her belly, Sammi managed to keep her words steady. "Rumors that you're sleeping with a cocktail waitress three weeks before the wedding are at odds with that impression, don't you think?"

Sammi held her breath, carefully watching his expression. Because those rumors would be nothing compared to the ones that'd explode if Sterling called off the wedding. She could just see the pitying looks and knowing nods. Those were the kind of rumors that could ruin a woman's life.

After a long moment, Sterling's remote expression shifted into a rueful smile.

"You're right. Totally right. That was my bad." He shrugged. "I promise, you won't hear any more gossip like that."

Sammi could only stare, and wonder. Did he mean he was done fooling around and that once they were married he'd only have sex with her? Or did he simply mean he'd be more careful about the gossip?

Before she could ask, they were greeted by a booming voice.

"Sterling, you old dog. And Sammi Jo. Aren't you a pretty thing." As big as his voice, Ben Martin grabbed a chair from an empty table and, without asking, joined them. "Gotta talk business, my friends. I hear you're looking for a discount on some long-term ads in the newspaper."

Sterling slid an apologetic look toward Sammi, then, of course, started talking business. She frowned at the irritation spiking through her system. It wasn't the first time one of their meals had been interrupted. Actually, it was rare that one wasn't. And it wasn't as if she could call Sterling out on his comment here in public.

She'd simply wait until after breakfast and go with Sterling to her office. They would talk in private. They'd hash it out and settle the issue like two reasonable adults. Because that's what they were. That's why they were marrying each other.

Some of the tension she'd been carrying since yesterday finally loosened in her shoulders as Sammi smiled her thanks as Darla set her huevos rancheros on the table. While the men talked business, she ate her breakfast while mentally rehearsing the best way to approach their discussion.

"Excuse me, Sammi Jo. Julio needs you in the kitchen." From the frantic edge to Darla's smile, Julio was having one of his tantrums. The man was simply not a good enough chef to be worth the drama, but Mr. Barclay insisted on keeping the guy.

"I'm sorry, gentlemen, but now my business calls," she said, rubbing her napkin over her lips before sliding to her feet.

"Nice chatting with you, Sammi Jo."

"I'll see you up in the office when you're finished," Sterling said, lifting his hand to squeeze hers before she left. Her heart warming at the sweet gesture, Sammi squared her shoulders and prepared to do battle with a spatula-wielding diva.

Two hours later, she'd handled the kitchen emergency, fixed the reservation snafu, checked in three guests and had approved housekeeping's request to call the repairman to look at the leaking washing machine.

And she still couldn't get into her office. The last time she'd tried, Sterling had growled from his position hunched over her computer. She stood at the top of the stairs, debating going into her office to try again, or down to the lobby to find busywork.

"There you are. Let's go to the bridal suite right away."

For a brief second, Sammi considered opening a side window and jumping. But she had a feeling that even broken bones wouldn't save her. Not bothering to hide her reluctance, she turned to face Mrs. Ross.

"This isn't a good time to discuss wedding plans. How about tomorrow." Or never.

"This can't wait for tomorrow. Come, come, let's do it now." Dressed in eye-searing orange, Mrs. Ross gestured for Sammi to hurry up. "This will only take a quarter of an hour."

Knowing the woman would nag her for longer than that, Sammy cast one last longing look toward her office where Sterling was probably still happily ensconced in front of her computer. Then, as she did with all distasteful things, she got on with getting it over.

As soon as she stepped into the still-being-remodeled bridal suite, her frown deepened to a scowl.

"What'd you do to my wedding dress? Did you cut it in half," Sammi exclaimed. But after a second, her scowl faded. About three-quarter length now, without the yards of petal-like chiffon layers it might be a lot easier to move in.

Relief battled joy. She liked it.

"Of course not. This is the second dress."

"Second... No." Sammi shook her head. "I'm not wearing two dresses."

Completely ignoring her, Mrs. Ross continued to roar around the room like a steamroller, bustling from the dress to her sewing basket and back again like a wide orange blur against the elegant blue room.

"You wear the formal one for the ceremony and after the first dance, this similar but less formal one for the reception." Seeing Sammi's mutinous expression, Mrs. Ross pursed her lips, then added, "Once I'd explained to Mr. Barclay that second dresses are all the trend, he agreed that it was a perfect idea."

Sammi eyed the dress, then the martinet with the measuring tape. She wanted to protest. She wanted to put her foot down. She wanted to elope, dammit. But Sterling's words about how important the wedding was rang in her ears. She unbuttoned her blouse.

"Tattoos are trendy, too," Sammi muttered as the woman helped her into the dress, then pinned and tucked. "Were you planning on just me getting one, or the entire wedding party?"

"Perfect." Mrs. Ross walked around Sammi ten minutes later, inspecting every inch. "The fit is just right. I have an idea for straps, though, for the more vigorous dancing. The fabric is in my car. Hold on. Don't move. I'll be right back."

And with that, she was gone.

Leaving Sammi trapped in her second dress.

She debated calling down for one of the staff to come unbutton her, but before she could decide if it was worth the inevitable drama, her cell phone rang from the pocket of her cargo pants.

"Sterling?" she answered with a laugh. "I thought you were just down the hall using my—"

"Sammi, listen," Sterling interrupted, his words an urgent rush. "Don't say anything, just listen to me."

"What's wrong? Sterling, are you okay?" Her stomach leaden with fear, Sammi dropped to the bed. The dress fluffed around her legs like small chiffon clouds.

"Look, something's come up. Something important." His voice choked for a moment, then, sounding as if he were in pain, he continued. "I'm going to be away for a few days. Maybe a week. You have to cover for me."

"What's going on?" Fear was bubbling to the surface now, threatening to choke her. She pushed off the bed and headed for the door. "I thought you were in my office. When did you leave?"

She rushed down the hall toward her office, stopping short at the sight of the mess. The chair lay on its side, one wheel missing. Papers covered her desk, looking as if they'd been thrown like confetti and her computer monitor flashed from black to blue and back again.

"Oh, my God," she breathed. "Sterling, are you in trouble? Should I call the police? I'm going to call your father."

"No!" His breath came over the line sounding as shaky as the nerves in Sammi's stomach. "Don't call anybody. That'll make it worse. Just do what I asked."

No way in hell.

Sammi didn't say a word, but apparently that was as good as declaring intent, because there was a scuffling sound.

"Prove it to her," she heard a mean voice order.

"Who is that? Where are you, Sterling?"

There was a grunt, then a wheezing sound. Sammi ran to the landline. She didn't care what he said. She was calling the cops.

"I'm switching to video call," Sterling said before she could lift the receiver. "Sammi, look at it."

With trembling fingers, she slowly pulled the phone away from her ear to look at the screen. And let out a small cry.

Sterling's face was bruised, his hair disheveled and his eyes filled with pleading. Her heart was trembling as hard as her hands now.

"Sammi—"

"Shut it."

Sterling shut it so fast, she saw his teeth snap together.

More scared to see how easily he acquiesced than she'd been already, Sammi tried to breathe through the panic. Her toes dug into the cool satin of her gilded wedding shoes, her fist clenched tight the fabric of her dress.

"Here's the deal," that same mean voice growled from offscreen. "You want him back, you do exactly what we say. You don't do it exactly, you won't be needing that pretty white dress."

The meaty hand shifted so the barrel of a gun pressed alongside Sterling's cheek.

"Yes," Sammi gasped. "Whatever you want. I'll do whatever you want."

"Don't tell anyone about this call. Don't tell anyone he's missing. You make damned sure that nobody has a clue." Already menacing, the voice lowered to send chills of terror down Sammi's spine. "If you don't, we'll know. And we'll make him pay."

"Listen to them," Sterling insisted, his expression showing the same apprehension Sammi felt. "Sammi, do exactly what they tell you. Just cover for me. Make excuses. Find a way to make sure that nobody questions my being away. If you can do that, everything will be okay."

"But—"

The cell phone went black. They'd ended the call. Sammi tried to breathe, but the panic kept bubbling up in her throat.

What was she supposed to do?

She couldn't just pretend everything was okay.

But what choice did she have?

Her head pounded in time with the black dots dancing in her eyes, her heart throbbing so fast, so loud, that she could barely breathe.

She wanted to call Mr. Barclay and beg him to fix this. To find his son, bring him back.

But the menacing warning still sounded in her ears, a loud and clear hissing threat that terrified her to her very core.

Sammi pressed her lips tight.

She couldn't tell Mr. Barclay.

They'd kill Sterling if she did.

But she couldn't just trust that it'd work out. That the creeps with the ugly guns would keep their promise. Why would they? What did they want with Sterling, anyway? Nothing good, she was sure. But if they wanted a ransom, why didn't they want Mr. Barclay to know?

Her head was spinning too fast for Sammi to find any of those answers. All she could do was lean against the wall and try to suck in air. She clenched the phone tight to her chest, but couldn't bring herself to call anyone. Not with the threats ringing so clearly in her head.

She had to do something.

Anything.

Then, out of the blue, she remembered.

Laramie was in town.

"You sure about this?"

"Yep." The bridle in one hand, Laramie gave the horse's neck a fond pat with the other before leading Storm out of the stable. Small dust clouds followed their steps through the scrubby grass toward the paddock where the sun beat down like hot spikes. Having served months in the Middle East, the heat barely registered on Laramie's radar, other than to make sure he had a decent supply of water for the ride.

"You could stay here. Just a day or two."

Checking his packs, Laramie slid a sideways glance at his uncle. The resemblance was there, but only if you knew to look for it. The shape of their eyes, although Laramie's were hazel instead of brown. The arch of their brow and the full lips. Art and his younger sister had shared those features. Features she'd passed on to her only son. Otherwise, Laramie was the spitting image of his father.

"What's wrong, Art?"

"Nothin's wrong. Just think maybe you shouldn't go up now. Go up next month instead."

Laramie frowned at the intensity in older man's voice. It wasn't as if this trip was out of the ordinary. He came back once a year to make this sort of pilgrimage from his uncle's spread outside of El Paso up to the family cabin in the mountains. But it was rare that he made it back the first week of June. It was just as rare that his uncle said anything about it, though.

Laramie came back because he was a part of this land. Even as a kid, all he'd wanted was to ride horses on the land he loved, go to school like a regular kid and sleep in the same bed night after night.

At twelve, he'd used his mom's love to force her to choose between staying in Jerrick or constantly uprooting her son to tag along in her husband's search for fame. To decide between staying in town near her brother who'd look out for her, in a place where there was steady work and a real school. Or to follow the rodeo circuit yet again, where their every meal and every mood depended on how long his father stayed in the saddle. Bottom line, he'd forced her to choose between him and his dad.

She'd chosen him.

Two years later, his father was dead of a broken neck and his mother of a broken heart.

So he knew why Art might think he was here out of guilt or some misplaced need to atone. But he'd be wrong.

"This is the time I was able to get leave," Laramie said, bothering to explain like he'd do for few people. "So this is when I'm heading up."

Expecting that to be the end of it, Laramie tucked one foot into the stirrup. Before he could swing his leg over the saddle, though, Art scurried forward, putting one hand on Storm's neck.

"Beatrice, she's been dead almost fifteen years now, Christian."

Settling both feet back on the ground, Laramie blinked at the unfamiliar use of his given name. He heard it so rarely now that it fit like a piece of clothing long outgrown.

"She'd be proud of you, Beatrice would. She'd want you to move on with your life."

Would she? For eleven months and one week out of every year, Laramie managed to put aside any and all thought of his mother, of his family, of his life before he'd joined the Navy. He wasn't a bitter man, nor was he running from his past. He was simply practical. The past was over. Gone. So remembering it was pointless.

But he owed the man in front of him too much to point that out. Art had opened his house to a troubled fourteen-year-old. He'd shown a boy with vague ambitions of being a rodeo bull rider to look past the stables, beyond the ranch. In his own gruff, taciturn way, Art had taught Laramie to live.

So no matter how impatient he was to be off, no matter how stupid he thought it was to waste time acting as if the past was no big deal, Laramie gave the old man his attention.

Because he owed him.

"I'm a Navy SEAL. I'm based in California when I'm not deployed elsewhere. I'm a debt-free, contributing member of society." Laramie paused, frowning at the hand-tooled stitching on the saddle, faded and worn after so many years. "What else is necessary for me to do in order to be considered having moved on?"

The bandy-legged old man frowned, the move creasing

his wrinkles even deeper. He scratched his fingers through the grizzled thatch of gray hair circling from ear to ear.

"I dunno. Maybe she'd expect you to be married by now or somethin'. A man hits thirty, he'd better think about the future."

"I'm doing just fine the way I am." Laramie grinned as he swung into the saddle, settling in as if it'd just been yesterday that he'd been on a horse instead of three hundred yesterdays.

He'd given Art the same answer last year, the year before, all the way back to his twenty-fourth year. The older man's attempt to do right by his sister was as much a part of the coming-home ritual as the ride to the cabin.

But as Laramie had told him time and time again, he was doing fine.

"See you in a few," Laramie said, tapping his fingers to the brim of his Stetson. Without looking back, he tapped his heels against the horse to signal a walk, waiting until he left Rolling Stone land to gallop, out of respect.

He took the meandering path without having to think about it. He simply rode. He'd spent most of his childhood at the cabin. As a family when his dad wasn't following the rodeo circuit. Just him and his mom most of the rest of the time.

He'd been happy there.

Until his mother had died there. Because he hadn't been able to save her.

That's why he went back every year.

Not out of guilt or a need to make amends. He hadn't done anything deserving of punishment. And even if he had, being orphaned was probably payment enough.

He followed the familiar terrain toward the mountains.

No. He didn't come back to punish himself.

He came back to remind himself.

Of who he was.

Of where he'd come from.

And of how far he'd come.

And of the fact that he'd never be helpless again.

That, he decided, leaning back in the saddle and letting peace settle over him, was as much of his thoughts as he was giving to Art's concerns. And like anything else Laramie put his mind to, he did just that. The concerns, the thoughts of having anything to prove, all of it was shoved right out of his head.

It took him an hour of easy riding with that clear head of his until he reached the clearing where the cabin was settled. A small one-story log building, the wide porch wrapped around toward the back where a narrow river babbled along. Laramie dismounted, tossed his gear on the porch and walked the horse toward its little home away from home for the next three weeks.

It took him longer to settle the horse in the lean-to with water and a scoop of grain than it did to settle his supplies in the cabin. All he had to do was toss his pack on the bed, and he was back outdoors.

It was tradition, not guilt that had Laramie heading along a narrow path toward the west. A few trees had fallen here and there, but the small, flower-filled clearing was the same as it always had been. Peaceful and serene. Beatrice had called it her Zen Zone.

He barely glanced at the simple headstone. There was no need. He'd commissioned it himself. Had carried it up on horseback and set it there over his mother's grave fifteen years past. He knew exactly what it said.

Beatrice Laramie. "To thine own self be true."

How often had he heard her say that? It was her one and only rule.

Art's words danced through his head, making Laramie grin again.

His mom had been all about truth to self, and she'd expect him to be married? No way.

As if mocking the thought, a rustling came from his left. Rocks clanked together and branches slapped at each other.

Laramie frowned.

It only took him a second to assess the situation. This was a pretty remote place. He was alone. Other than stocking the food supplies, Art didn't come up here and didn't expect to hear from him for three weeks. And there was no cell service. On the asset list, he knew there was a shotgun in the cabin and rope in the lean-to. And, of course, his own skills.

Grinning as much in battle anticipation as to welcome the distraction, Laramie dropped into a crouch, his hands fisted and his eyes trained on the rustling bush.

A second later, a five-foot-ten mass in cream satin burst through the foliage.

The sight damn near knocked him on his ass.

Thankfully, he had good balance.

So Laramie was able to straighten and reassess at the same time without losing more than a dozen or so brain cells.

Luckily the brain cells trained to assess and evaluate the female form were still working just fine. The golden complexion lent truth to the fact that the disheveled red hair falling from the knot atop her head to float around her shoulder was natural.

He considered himself an expert on the female form, so he knew his evaluation of her body as damned good was spot-on. Broad shoulders rose above lightly muscled arms, and as she straightened to better pull those deep breaths down to her belly, he gave a silent hum of appreciation.

Oh yeah, she had a sweet body. Fabric cupped breasts full enough to fill both his hands, then wrapped snugly around a long torso, slender waist and narrow hips. From there down she was a mystery because of the ocean of material, but based on the facts on hand, Laramie had to believe that the legs would be as much a turn-on as the rest of her.

For a brief second, he had to wonder if Art had been more serious than he'd figured about that last suggestion. Laramie wouldn't put it past him, but he just couldn't figure where the old man would find a woman this hot to play the part.

Which meant she was probably lost or running from something.

As hard as it was to tear his eyes from the striking face with its razor-sharp cheekbones, slashing brows and full lips, Laramie managed to cast his eyes behind her.

He checked the bushes to the left.

He scanned the trees to the right.

His slowed breath quieted his heartbeat. The only sounds around were the light rustling of the wind in the trees and the light panting from the sexy redhead.

Laramie waited another few seconds, his senses attuned for footfalls, engines, anything that'd hint that there were more people around.

Nothing.

So he lifted his Stetson off the branch where he'd hung it, setting it back on his head and angling the brim just so.

And took another look.

This time he smiled.

Under the gloss and glamour, he knew that face.

She liked grape popsicles on hot summer days, preferred crayons to paints and had a penchant for standing up to bullies.

"Hello, Sammi Jo," he drawled.

"Laramie. Hi." The bride bent from the waist again with both hands pressed to her belly as she tried to catch her breath. After a couple of attempts, she shrugged as if acknowledging that it just wasn't going to happen. Instead, she gave him an arch look and said in just as breathless a voice,

"You said you'd help if I ever needed it. Remember? Well, I need your help."

4

LARAMIE DIDN'T EXACTLY look thrilled to see her, but who could blame him? Sammi didn't know too many single guys who'd be thrilled to be chased down by a woman in a wedding dress. Even fewer who were crazy about someone they hadn't seen in a dozen years crashing their vacation with a plea for help.

Sammi Jo watched him pace in front of a fireplace that took up an entire wall of the cabin, the rough-hewn stone a gray backdrop against his long lean body.

Even irritated, he moved with a sensual sort of grace. The kind that made Sammi think he'd move like that in bed. So smooth, but with determination that said he always got exactly where he wanted to go.

Like a silk-covered jackhammer.

Like most of the men in Jerrick, Laramie wore a plaid flannel shirt over his T, jeans and cowboy boots. But the standard cowboy uniform looked so different on him.

Perched on the buffalo-hide couch, Sammi narrowed her eyes. It could be that the back pocket of his jeans had no white ring from carrying a can of chewing tobacco. Her eyes followed his backside as he paced the other way, noting that the denim decorated one very nice butt. Her hands warmed with the urge to pat it. Just to check and see if it was as firm as it looked.

As horrified as if she'd said that aloud instead of in her head, Sammi ripped her gaze from Laramie's backside. It landed on his shoulders, covered in blue-striped black fabric and broad enough to hold two full-grown women. Or for one to hang on to during sexy times.

No wonder he was a sexual legend in Jerrick.

She took a deep breath, trying to settle the weird feeling in her stomach. Dancing butterflies? Wild dragons? Horny hop toads, more likely.

Oh, my.

Sammi dropped her head into her hands, pressing her fingers against her eyes in an attempt to clear the crazies. What was she doing? Her fiancé was in danger, and here she was having her first ever lusting thoughts about the man she'd come to ask to find him.

What was happening to her? Had stress unhinged something in her DNA? Was this how her mama had started? Stress-induced lust? Maybe it was a vicious circle, with the lust then causing stress that caused more lust until next thing you knew, you were doing the ice-cream truck driver to get an extra scoop.

"Sammi Jo? Hey now, don't cry."

He sounded as horrified as if she'd set his Stetson on fire. Laramie stopped pacing so fast, she heard his boots skid on the plank floor.

But when she lifted her head to assure him that she wasn't crying, he didn't look horrified. He looked as if he wanted to toss her out the door onto her wedding-dress-covered butt. Then the thought of Mrs. Ross's face if he did popped into her head and suddenly, her eyes did fill with tears.

"Stop that." He gave a sharp shake of his head. "You let one tear drop and I'm walking out that door."

"It's your cabin," she pointed out, the urge to laugh doing more to waylay her hysteria-fueled tears than his threat.

"Then I'll make you go." As he looked her over, his frown deepened so that she noticed the grooves bracketing his mouth and creasing his brow. The lines were well-worn, as if he frowned a lot. But that was so at odds with Laramie's reputation as an easygoing, love 'em and leave 'em smiling kind of guy that she almost dismissed the idea. Almost. Because, well, the grooves were there.

The urge to find out what had put them there was so strong that Sammi leaned back a little. As if those two inches would keep her from getting too personal.

"Look, don't take this wrong, Sammi, but I'm here to relax." As if challenging her two-inch safety zone, he closed the distance between them, squatting down in front of where she sat. He smelled like the outdoors. Warm, free and just a little wild. The scent was so tempting, Sammi wanted to lean in and nuzzle her face against his throat and breathe him in. Instead, she tried to subtly breathe through her teeth. "If you had second thoughts two steps from the altar, well good job seeing the trap and getting the hell out. If you already said *I do*, then I'm sorry. I'm not available for jealousy games."

What sort of games was he available for? She could feel the words as they danced on the tip of her tongue, hear their flirtatious tone.

Sammi wanted to drop her head into her hands again and try to massage some sense back into her brain. But Laramie was so close she was afraid to move in case she accidentally touched him. Who knew what'd happen then.

She might spontaneously orgasm. She'd heard friends say it could happen.

Then she replayed the rest of his words.

Wait. Jealousy game? What was he talking about? Oh… Sammi glanced down at the white skirt fluffing around her like petals.

"Oh, no—" She started to explain that she wasn't married yet. That she'd been in the middle of a fitting and hadn't taken the time to change.

But Laramie stopped her words with just a single shake of his head.

"I hate to deny a beautiful, sexy woman anything." His voice deepened, his gold-rimmed hazel eyes sliding over her like a caress, leaving tingles in its path. "But darlin', I have a couple of rules I live my life by. One of them is to never fool around with married women. Not even as a favor to help them make their husband jealous."

"Isn't that awfully cynical," she dismissed with a shake of her head.

"Experience begets cynicism."

"You're telling me that women—married and otherwise— have shown up at your place with the sole purpose of using you to make their significant other jealous?" That was crazy.

"Yep." He waited a beat, then added, "And to have sex."

And just like that, Sammi's body heated up again. She wet her lips, trying to ignore it.

"The married ones, too?"

"Yep."

She wanted to ask him how often it happened. Did he only refuse to have sex with the married ones? A million questions ran through Sammi's mind, many of them accompanied by images. For a woman who had previously had virtually no interest in sex, Sammi was feeling a little overwhelmed. And hot. She resisted the urge to wave her hand to try to cool herself off.

She stared at Laramie, who was staring right back at her. His face was actually beautiful. Sculpted cheekbones and full lips went with the sharp angles of his chin, while his magnetic eyes were topped with brows a few shades darker than his toffee-colored hair.

That hair was short, whereas the last time she'd seen him, it'd been long enough to blow in the breeze. Still, her fingers itched to touch it. To see if it was sharp or soft.

Why was she here, again?

Sterling. *Dammit.* Sammi mentally smacked herself. Sterling.

"Look you've got it wrong. I'm not..." She blinked. "You think I'm sexy?"

"You just got that part, huh?" His smile flashed, sending a hot shard of desire to lodge deep in Sammi's belly.

"I'm not usually slow on the uptake," she said, disliking the idea of Laramie thinking she'd grown up into a bubblehead. Unable to sit any longer, Sammi pushed to her feet.

Laramie took her place on the couch—looking much more comfortable than she had with his arm stretched along the back and his ankle resting on his knee while Sammi took over pacing in front of the fireplace.

"It's been a weird day, okay? Sterling was a total grump at breakfast, then he took my computer. Which left me nowhere to hide from the second wedding dress. Who needs two dresses for one wedding, I ask you?"

Since she really was clueless, she threw her hands in the air as she paced.

"Two questions."

The words were barely louder than a murmur, but they stopped Sammi in her tracks.

"Okay?"

"First, you're marrying Sterling Barclay?"

"You know Sterling?" Her stomach tightened again at the thought of her fiancé and what he might be going through now. A part of her wanted to blurt out a plea, to beg and scream for help. But her logical side—usually in complete command—had argued during her frantic drive to the cabin that she needed to lay it all out clearly.

Laramie was so used to women throwing emotions all over him, he was probably immune. But logic, that was smart and reasonable. So he'd respond in the same way.

"Let's see," Laramie mused, easing his hat further back on his head. "Uptight pinhead who liked fancy cars and wore his letterman jacket like a badge of honor. Had a penchant for cheating and always hid behind daddy's name."

Oh. Sammi bit her lip. Well, that wasn't good. That sort of opinion could make persuading Laramie to rescue Sterling a little more challenging.

"You said two things?" she reminded him, buying time. Sterling had gone to a private school, so what had given Laramie those impressions? How did she change them without knowing?

"Two, you keep moving around like that and you're gonna pop right out of that dress." His smile went from easygoing to wicked in a flash. "Not that I mind. The view promises to be a good one. Just thought you'd want to know."

Sammi's arms dropped to her sides so fast, her wrists bounced on her hips.

"Yeah. That's what I thought."

Even as it made her want to giggle, the look on his face, a sort of heated intensity, derailed her thoughts once again.

"So what's the deal?" No longer teasing, his expression turned serious, his eyes watchful. "Are you in trouble? Running from someone?"

"No, not me. I'm fine," she hurried to assure him. As the iced fury faded in his eyes, she felt something soften in her heart. Appreciation, she told herself. She'd never had anyone willing to defend her before.

Except Laramie himself, of course.

But it had a lot bigger impact now that he was all grown up. Her gaze wandered again, meandering a slow path over those broad, strong shoulders, down that chest—so muscular that she could see definition beneath his black T-shirt—and down toward his belt.

That's enough. She forced her eyes back upward again. She'd confirmed that he was all grown-up. No need to check the particulars.

"So, here's the deal," she blurted, needing to start her spiel before she got distracted by particulars again. "I'm getting married."

"No, really?"

Sammi rolled her eyes. Then, because he'd interrupted she had to start her carefully rehearsed request from the top.

"I'm getting married. To Sterling Barclay." She waited, but when there were no derogatory comments or change in Laramie's expression, she relaxed her shoulders and continued. "The wedding is in three weeks. Well, two weeks and five days now, actually. So there's a lot going on. Preparations for the wedding and for after the wedding and all sorts of changes at the inn."

Laramie arched his brow.

"Oh, I'm assistant manager at the Barclay Inn." She paused, just in case he wanted to offer congratulations or anything. But Laramie simply stared. That intense, penetrating stare. "Remember? The Barclay Inn. I was all set to run away that summer when I was fifteen. I even asked you for a ride to the bus station. You talked me out of it, took me to the inn and convinced the housekeeper, Mrs. Reed, to give me a job even though I wasn't old enough."

She bit her lip, afraid she'd start babbling if he didn't say something soon. As if hearing her thoughts and willing to prevent that, he finally nodded.

"I remember."

Oh, God. It was the pained look in his eyes that made her want to groan. The reason he'd had so much pull with the housekeeper was because Laramie's mom had worked there right up until she died. And here Sammi was reminding him of that.

She had to swallow hard to get past the knot in her throat.

"So, um, Sterling and I are engaged. And we meet for breakfast on Tuesdays and Thursdays, so we met this morning as usual," she explained, trying to find her rhythm again. "What?"

His hand resting on his knee, Laramie had raised one finger.

"Do I need to know this?"

Sammi rolled her eyes.

"I don't know. Why don't I tell you and then we can decide." She'd worked so hard on what she'd say and how she'd say it, and she needed to mention every point. After all, she didn't know which one would be most persuasive and she couldn't afford to skip a single one.

But the tone of Laramie's question made it clear that he wasn't impressed with any of the points so far. What if he refused to help her? Sammi thought of how long it'd been since that phone call. Her heart shuddered, stomach cramping tight against the worry she'd so carefully tucked away. The only thing that'd kept her from hysterics so far was the promise that she'd find Laramie and he'd help her. But now that promise was crumbling.

"They kidnapped Sterling," she blurted out.

Laramie's only reaction was to narrow his eyes.

"Someone took him. They're threatening him. They could kill him." With each word her voice rose a smidge higher on the hysteria scale.

"Why don't you go back to breakfast."

Bent at the waist, Sammi Jo paused in the act of sucking in great big gulps of air to give Laramie a questioning look through the wavy strands of hair hanging in her face.

"I beg your pardon?"

When Laramie circled his finger in the air, Sammi took it to mean he'd decided that he did need to know. She was too worried about Sterling to smirk. Much.

"Sterling and I had breakfast at the inn, as we do every Tuesday and Thursday and afterward he closed himself in my office. He was still there two hours later when Mrs. Ross cornered me into trying on this second wedding dress."

"You planning on marrying more than one guy?"

"Ha. No. Apparently it's some crazy trend. Probably thought up by dress designers and bridezillas unwilling to get past their special day." Unable to stand still with all the tension winding through her body, Sammi started pacing again. Her toes ached from too much time in her pointy-toed heels, but she walked through the pain. "So I'm trying on this dress and arguing with the wedding coordinator about needing more than one when my phone rang."

Sammi could see it in her mind as if she were there. Mrs. Ross in eye-searing orange, the scent of the beeswax polish used to polish the hall floor that morning. Her irritation, both at Mrs. Ross and at Sterling for messing up her day.

There she'd been, thinking about herself and her oh-so-justified irritation while poor Sterling was being kid-napped. Hurt. Possibly worse.

Greasy fingers of panic slid up Sammi's throat, grab-bing and squeezing. Her ears rang with the sound of bells dancing on the ocean.

"Cell or landline?"

Sammi had to blink to clear the tiny black dots from her vision before she could frown at him.

"What?"

"We'll get back to it. Before you pass out, why don't you tell me exactly what was said on the call."

"I'm not going to pass out."

Could he be any less sympathetic? Sammi actually felt her bottom lip slide out. He'd been a lot more helpful when he was seven, rescuing her from bullies. She'd bet if she passed out now, he'd simply watch her fall.

After a quick glance at the light coat of dust carpeting the hardwood floor, Sammi dropped onto the couch, mak-ing sure to sit as far from Laramie as she could.

"The call," she said slowly, playing it back though her mind. Her burning eyes focused on the toes of her fancy wedding shoes, Sammi repeated everything she could re-member about the conversation. She'd memorized the call time. She told him about the threats and demands. Her voice shook when she described how scared Sterling had looked and the bruises on his face.

"They said not to go to the cops, not to tell Mr. Barclay, nothing," she said as she reached the end of her recitation. Only then did she lift her eyes from her satin-covered feet to look at Laramie.

He wasn't looking at her. Eyes half closed, he'd slid into a slouch and with his hat tilted low like it was, looked dan-gerously close to falling asleep.

Sammi's foot tapped the floor, her fingers keeping silent

time on her knee. She knew this probably wasn't nearly as big and dangerous and exciting as the stuff he did as a SEAL, but dammit, couldn't he at least stay awake long enough to advise her on how to rescue her fiancé?

She'd yell, beg or try to shake a response out of him, but Sammi knew better. She'd grown up around enough cowboys to know it was pointless. He'd talk when he was ready.

But as hard as she tried to stop them, her eyes kept straying back to the man sitting on the couch.

He really was gorgeous. She felt as if she were sitting next to a live current of energy, but instead of lighting a room if plugged in, it'd make a body explode in pleasure.

She jumped back to her feet, hurrying across the room. Just in case.

And wondered what the hell was he thinking?

WHAT THE HELL had he been thinking?

Coulda stayed at Art's and had a beer, *but no*. Coulda spent last night with one or both of the barflies and caught a later flight, *but no*. Coulda taken the long trail through the national park, *but no*.

He'd just had to stick with tradition.

Laramie drummed his fingers on his knee and wondered if he should drop and do a hundred pushes for forgetting one of the key points of Basic Underwater Demolition/SEAL training. Habits got people killed.

Or worse.

He eyed the sultry redhead standing next to the fireplace chewing on her thumbnail. She'd definitely grown into the promise she'd shown as a kid with a mile of long legs and huge soulful eyes. Despite the worry lines creasing her brow, the fact that she was wearing a wedding dress and the twig wedged in her russet waves, Sammi Jo

Wilson looked pretty damned good for a walking, talking time bomb.

Sammi must've been around seven or eight when he'd first made her acquaintance. She'd been trying to hold her own in a fight with three other kids when Laramie had stepped in to even the numbers. Something to this day he wasn't sure had really been necessary. But even then, he'd been a sucker for playing hero.

His mistake hadn't been in stepping in, Laramie reminded himself. After the brats had been dispatched with their bullying tails between their legs, he'd asked Sammy why they'd been picking on her.

Red hair tangled around a face dusted with dirt, her lip split and knuckles raw, she'd lifted that chin of hers and told him that it was none of his damned business. Laramie remembered laughing and, being too dumb a kid to let it go, asking a few more times.

But even that hadn't been his mistake.

Nope, the mistake was upon hearing Sammi's whispered confession that she couldn't read—that she was afraid if the teacher realized that, Child Protective Services would take her away from her home—Laramie had taken that hero thing a little too seriously.

And had offered to teach her himself.

He'd often thought in the months after that he should have just kept on walking, instead of stepping into that fight.

Letting the memories roll over him, Laramie watched Sammi shift from foot to foot, her impatience building.

"Please," she said, her tone somewhere between pleading and threatening. "Say something."

Laramie's lips twitched. She'd held out about thirty seconds longer than he'd figured she would. That was something to admire—a woman with staying power.

But when the woman was Sammi Jo Wilson, he knew that staying power doubled as muleheaded stubbornness.

But no matter how stubborn she was or how much that sexy upper lip of hers appealed to him, she wasn't dragging him into her fight.

Not this time.

"I'm guessing over the last dozen years, you didn't forget how to read."

Her brows, shades darker than her hair, drew together. A faint wash of apricot colored her cheeks.

"Of course not," she said, choosing her words carefully as if sensing a trap.

Smart girl. Laramie smiled.

"Then you shouldn't have had any problem understanding that sign on the road you passed on your way up here."

"I'm not trespassing," she insisted with a roll of her eyes. "You're the one who invited me into your cabin. Sure you grunted, sighed and pointed your thumb toward the front door. But it was still an invitation."

Yeah. She was probably right about that. Laramie pushed to his feet and sauntered to what his mother had optimistically called the kitchen. The old Wedgewood stove took up most of one wall, the chipped cast iron a dull white against the rough-hewn wood walls. The squat, 50s-era refrigerator was creased on the side where Laramie had fallen headfirst into it when he was nine. A granite-topped wine barrel and two sawed-off tree trunks made up the dining table.

He ignored all of that to grab a beer from the nice modern cooler Art had left here for him. Still bent over his two-week supply, he tilted the bottle toward Sammi in question.

And took her fists-on-her-hip growl as a no.

Straightening, he closed the cooler with his knee at the same time he twisted the cap free.

"Laramie, I need your help. Now, if you don't mind, before something worse happens to Sterling."

Not taking his eyes off her, Laramie lifted the bottle to his lips and drank as he considered how to say no.

He had no doubt that whatever trouble Sterling Barclay had gotten himself into, he deserved. The guy had been an ass all his childhood, he'd been an ass the last time Laramie had seen him thirteen years ago. He had no doubt the man was still an ass.

But it wasn't Sterling Barclay asking for his help. And there'd always been something about Sammi that made it impossible to flat-out refuse her. He had to work his way around to it.

"Look, Sammi, if you really want him back," he paused, shrugging when she gave him a wide-eyed nod, "Then you need someone trained in that. Call the cops."

"They told me they'd hurt Sterling if I called a cop."

"If you're not willing to bring the police into this," he continued in the same tone even as he wondered how a woman could look so furiously stubborn and so damned sexy at the same time. "Take it to his father. The old man has connections. Let him take care of it."

There.

Considering the matter settled, Laramie tipped back the bottle to finish his beer.

"Absolutely not. First off, Sterling called me, not his father. I'm sure he has reasons for not wanting Mr. Barclay involved in this," Sammi said with a determined jut of her chin. "If you won't help me, I'll find a way to rescue Sterling myself."

"That's a good way to get yourself hurt."

"If that's what it takes." She gave a sharp nod. Her bottom lip was trembling, but he could see the determination in her eyes.

She'd do it.

Laramie clenched his jaw.

She'd find a way to jump into the middle of whatever clusterfuck of a mess that idiot Barclay had made and get herself seriously hurt—or worse, depending on how much stupider the man had gotten over the years.

In a rare show of temper, Laramie threw the bottle in the trashcan under the sink, the velocity intense enough to shatter the glass, sending shards across the floor. All year long, he could roll with whatever came his way. He handled enemy fire, exploding mountains, catfights and irritating warrant officers, all with ease.

But these three weeks, this cabin, they were his, dammit.

He scowled at Sammi, who hadn't flinched or frowned at his nasty little display. Whether it was a credit to her strength of nerve or simply a byproduct of being brought up by a crazy bitch like Cora Mae was a toss-up.

"Are you going to help me?" she asked quietly, those moss-green eyes of hers a liquid plea. Her moves slow and hesitant, as if she were approaching a wild animal, Sammi crossed the room until she stood a few inches from him. She was tall enough to meet his eyes, her body curvy enough that a deep breath would bring them into hot, tempting contact. "Please, Laramie."

She reached out, laying one slender hand on his arm. Her fingers burned through his shirt, searing his flesh with need.

Laramie studied the woman in front of him the same way he'd study a bomb he was supposed to disarm.

With determination, respect and a great deal of caution.

"If I help, it's on my terms," he heard himself say, the words hitting his brain as if coming from a long distance. Not surprising since reckless crazy wasn't exactly something he was used to.

"Whatever you want," she promised in a voice as giddy as her smile was relieved. She wrapped her hands around his now, lifting them together as if in prayer. "Anything."

Anything.

Laramie gave a slight shake of his head as he wondered how the hell she'd ended up so innocent given everything she'd seen over the years.

"My terms," he repeated. "That means you let me deal with this my way, without question. Whether you agree or not, whether you understand why or whether you don't, it doesn't matter. You go along."

That was the way a military operation ran. That was how he worked. If she didn't like it, well the door was right there. But like it or not, Sammi only nodded.

"I'll do whatever it takes to get Sterling back safely," she agreed. Then, damn them both, she reached out to lay one hand against his chest.

The heat seared, need stirred.

Without taking a step he moved closer to Sammi's lush body.

Laramie liked to live as free as possible, figuring the fewer rules, the less he had to worry about.

But one of his few hard-and-fast rules was that married women were off-limits. And engaged and running around in a wedding dress was close enough to marriage to put Sammi in that category.

But he wanted her.

Shocked at that realization, he watched the rise and fall of those luxurious breasts covered in white lace and felt the need throb in time with her every inhalation.

"Don't say I didn't warn you."

Then, because rules or not, he simply had to taste her, Laramie leaned down and took her mouth.

5

WELL, DAMN.

Laramie was trained well enough to recognize danger when he felt it. And all the signals were there.

The tight pull in his gut.

The icy finger down his spine.

And, of course, the alarm bells jangling in his head.

He recognized it. He acknowledged it.

And he went right on ignoring it.

To do otherwise would mean pulling his mouth away from Sammi Jo's, and he wasn't about to do that.

She tasted too good.

She was as sweet as warm, spiced peaches and as tempting as a welcome sign, inviting him to come on in and enjoy.

Her lips were full, that delicate overbite too tempting not to nibble at. Her indrawn breath slid like silk over his mouth, making Laramie want to dive deeper.

But he held back.

Instead, his lips slid, hot and wet, over hers. Back and forth. Soft at first, then harder, firmer.

In Laramie's experience—which was pretty damned extensive—all it took was a kiss to know how a woman liked her sex. Hot and demanding? Softly passive? Hungry desperation? He'd felt them all.

But Sammi... Oh, God, Sammi.

She was all of that and more.

She was delicious.

Even as she let him set the pace, her fingers dug into his arms with a demanding bite. The hunger was there, he knew it. It'd be so easy to coax it free, to offer her more. To give her enough pleasure that she'd welcome everything he could offer.

But this was Sammi Jo, that rarely heard-from little voice chimed in the back of his mind. The kid he'd looked out for. The waif he'd taught to read.

No matter how good she felt, there were too many reasons why taking this further was a mistake. Their history, her fiancé, the fact that he was in his yearly no-sex zone, were just a few.

Then, as if hearing his thoughts and determined to challenge his control, Sammi shifted closer. She traced her tongue along the seam of his mouth, as if asking him to come out and play. Her body angled down the length of his so her breasts were cushioned against his chest and her thighs straddled one of his.

Dammit.

She was too tempting to resist.

Despite the multiple warnings flashing through his mind, Laramie slipped his tongue into her mouth for a taste. Hot and moist, it was like dipping his tongue into heaven.

Her moan trembled against his lips and sent a shaft of pleasure through Laramie so strong that he automatically reached down to cup her butt through all that fluffy material. He pulled her closer, pressing her tight against his throbbing erection.

As their tongues tangled together in a dance of desire his hands skimmed up the fullness of her cheek, along the sweet curve of the small of her back where the fluff gave way to rough lace. Ignoring the urgings from his dick, he carefully avoided touching the silky temptation of her bare skin, instead tangling his hands in her hair. The heavy strands felt like silken threads around his fingers, too soft for him to care that they were tying him in knots.

Her hands teased their way up his chest, the move both siren sexy and seductively sweet until she reached the collar of his shirt. She curled her hands tight behind his neck, as if trying to keep him from pulling away.

As if.

Every move he made, she mirrored.

Laramie's body tightened with desire as familiar to him as breathing. The need, though, was new.

It was unfamiliar enough to force him to pull back, to heed the warnings in his head. To back the hell off before he did something...

What? Laramie wondered as he slowly lifted his mouth from hers, waiting for Sammi to open her eyes.

What could be so bad about giving in to the passion flaming between them?

Her breath was shaky, her breasts pressed in tight temptation against his chest as Sammi Jo slowly opened her eyes. Her lashes were a silky dark fringe, shielding her eyes for a moment before she met his gaze.

The stunned delight in those moss-green depths fed his ego, made him grin. As Laramie's hands cupped her hips, his smile slowly slid away. Because beneath the delight was a hint of fear that he could have ignored, and passion-fueled curiosity.

The sort of curiosity that said that she'd be open to just

about anything—no matter how wild and kinky—that he might suggest they try.

"Sugar, you might not want to look at me that way."

"What way?" The words were a breathy drawl, her eyes slumberous as they focused on his mouth.

"The way that says you'd be happy to drop that second wedding dress of yours and let me have my way with your body." His voice lowered to a growl. "I'd show you things you've never imagined, Sammi Jo. I'd do things to you that you've never contemplated. And I'd make you like every one of them."

There. That should scare her.

But Sammi Jo didn't back off.

Instead, her smile widened, slow and curious.

"What kind of things?"

Laramie could only laugh.

With a shake of his head, he set her away from him as carefully as if she were an IED. Then, for good measure since he didn't have body armor, he took a couple steps back.

"Fine. Don't tell me." She'd find out for herself, Sammi's expression said.

Even as he mourned the loss of his comfortable, beer-buzzed sabbatical routine, Laramie wondered why he was saying no. She wasn't married. Her fiancé was a douche who'd probably skipped out instead of facing his responsibilities. And, more important, she had about the hottest mouth he'd ever kissed.

Still…

"Some things, Sammi Jo, you're better off not knowing."

WELL, DIDN'T THAT beat all.

Here she was, sexually aroused and seriously horny for the first time in her life, and the man responsible was telling her no.

Her breath still coming fast, Sammi stared at Laramie. She felt as if something inside her had melted away, leaving her exposed and unsure. A part of her wanted to grab hold of him, to plaster herself against his body and demand that he relieve these feelings churning deep inside her.

And if he wouldn't relieve them, then dammit, couldn't he at least tell her what they were? Was it technique? The dusty mountain air circulating the cabin? Did Laramie have exclusive dibs on whatever it was?

Sammi pressed her hands to her stomach, wishing she could ease the nerves jumping there. Her heart was racing just as fast and it felt as if her blood were on fire.

How'd he done that?

More importantly, why?

She watched as he strode back into the kitchen to pull another drink from the cooler, this time a bottle of water. Sunshine danced through the narrow window to spark gold streaks over his hair, lighting his face as he gulped down the water.

Sammi wet her lips as she watched his throat work, wondering how something so mundane could be sexy. It had to be Laramie. She'd seen hundreds of guys drink from a bottle over the years, and not one had ever made her want to beg for a taste. Until now.

"What was that for?" She had to swallow—twice—because her throat was so dry the words were sticking there. "Why did you kiss me?"

"You're a smart girl, Sammi Jo. You figure it out," he challenged, a hint of irritation riding on the words.

Shoulders twitching defensively, Sammi leaned against the back of the couch. Arms crossed over her chest, she welcomed the annoyance moving through her, pushing away the heat.

"Was that payment?" Her words were brittle, even as

her chin lifted. "A little something you wanted in return for your help?"

She'd thought she'd come to terms with her upbringing. That she'd moved past the drama of dragging around blame and regret. But as bitterness burned away the last of the pleasure-filled fog clouding her mind, Sammi had to admit she might have been wrong.

Folding her hands around themselves, she tried to hold the pain there, squeezing it away. So many times she felt that burning slap of disdain in her life. Even now, after years of distancing herself from her mother, even with the country-club polish and the gilt-stamped approval of marrying into the most influential family in the county, she felt it.

But maybe she deserved that disdain, a little voice whispered. Here she was, churned up and turned on by a man who wasn't her fiancé. What did that say about her?

"You want to clarify that question?" Laramie asked, tossing his empty bottle into a bucket before glancing back at her. Except for the irritation in his eyes, his expression could be termed neutral. Still, it sent a shiver of trepidation down her spine.

But Sammi didn't back down.

"I want to know if you think I'm going to have sex with you in return for you helping me find Sterling?"

There. Couldn't get any clearer than that.

"You're kidding, right?" Laramie said, the irritation in his eyes replaced by laughter. "Sugar, I'm a highly-skilled military machine. My training alone is worth more money than this entire town. You think you can pay me off with a kiss?"

Well, she'd actually thought the payment might be a lot more than just kissing. Feeling like an idiot and wondering where she'd made the wrong turn, assumption-wise, Sammi opened her mouth to apologize.

Laramie stopped her with a simple shake of his head.

"If anyone else said something like that to me, I'd be mighty pissed. I don't barter with sex, Sammi Jo. I don't have to." He waited a beat as the heat worked its way up Sammi's cheeks, then nodded. "Keep that in mind. Because when we do have sex, you're going to be the one asking."

Her mouth dropped.

She wanted to laugh. To say that that'd never happen. But as her stomach pitched into her toes, tingling the entire way, it assured Sammi that yes, given the chance, she should be very careful.

Otherwise she was going to be in big trouble.

Big, naked trouble.

"I came here for your help." She said, the words as much for her as for him. "I'm not here to sample your legendary sexual skills."

She tried for a contemptuous laugh, but given that her words were shaky and her laugh breathless, she didn't think she pulled it off. Not that she could tell from Laramie's expression. He was impossible to read.

His eyes were distant and that tempting mouth—still glistening from where she'd stroked it with her tongue—was hard.

"I guess we'll see where that goes," was all he said.

Sammi wanted to growl.

Or better yet, to scream. Why didn't he react to her insult? Why didn't he say something so she could be angry instead of churned up with needs she didn't understand?

"In the meantime, you might want to consider that you're not getting the whole picture."

Of course she wasn't. The picture was distorted by the

fact that he was wearing clothes. She didn't know how so many women did that imagining a guy naked thing. She couldn't seem to get past his belt buckle. Was he smooth or hair roughened? And how big was he down there, *really*? The rumors of his kissing were obviously true. Did that mean the rest of the gossip was, too?

If so, how the hell did it fit?

Her thighs constricted tight as she tried to imagine it, Sammi realized just exactly where her thoughts had gone. Horrified, she pressed her fingers against her temples. *Focus*, she ordered herself.

The last thing she should be thinking about when her fiancé was missing was the size of another man's equipment, dammit.

"What else is there to consider?" she asked. Her eyes rounded as the thought of kidnapping plots, political machinations and nefarious motivations ran through her mind. "Should I have Mr. Barclay watched? Do you think someone is after the whole family?"

"I'm sure the old man is just fine. What you should be wondering about is the possibility that your husband-to-be might not want you trying to *rescue* him."

Puzzled by the odd emphasis he'd put on rescue, Sammi shook her head.

"Of course he does. Why else would he have called me?"

Then, with jaw-dropping shock, it hit her.

"You think he skipped out to avoid our wedding? That he staged some elaborate kidnapping because he wanted to get out of marrying me?"

"Plenty of guys get cold feet."

A roaring filled Sammi's ears as the room did a swift three-sixty. She gripped the couch with stiff fingers, as much to ground herself as to keep from falling on her face.

Instead of looking at Laramie, she stared out the window with burning eyes as the idea filled her mind.

All her life, she'd pursued two goals. Respectability, and to stay off the gossips' radar. Oh, how those would both be shot to hell if this were true.

She could hear it now. The tut-tutting at the church social about that poor Wilson girl, getting what she deserved for aiming above her station. The pitying looks from employees at the inn as they wondered whether or not to accept her authority. Oh, god, the men. They'd start swarming again, figuring she was a younger version of Cora Mae.

How much would that suck?

A lot, Sammi admitted with a deep breath. But nothing had changed. Well, given that she'd discovered the questionable delight of inappropriate lust, she had to admit that she'd changed. But nothing pertaining to her reason for coming had changed. Whether he'd orchestrated it or not, Sterling was missing. And she had to find him, if for no other reason than his disappearance would break Mr. Barclay's heart.

Her gaze shifted back to Laramie, who was leaning against the refrigerator, looking as if he might take a nap.

"Are you going to help me find Sterling?" she asked quietly.

His expression remote, undecipherable, Laramie finally nodded.

"Give me your cell phone," he said, holding out one hand.

"My phone?" Sammy automatically reached for her pocket before remembering that she was wearing a wedding dress, it had no pockets and her phone wasn't with her. "I left it in the truck."

She frowned when she saw the impatient look on his face.

"You have no cell service up here," she pointed out. "And I have nowhere to put a phone. It was easier to leave it. Besides, I already tried that GPS tracking thing, but it has to be on both phones. Sterling doesn't have his on."

Laramie pushed away from the fridge and headed for the door.

"Where are you going?" Sammi straightened, starting after him.

"To get your phone."

LARAMIE COULD TURN a cell phone into a bomb. He could alter one to connect with a military satellite and, if necessary, he could turn one into a jammer to disrupt enemy radio signals. But his knowledge of electronics wasn't extensive enough to hack into one and figure out a caller's location.

His expertise was explosives.

And he was smart enough to recognize a volatile situation when he was standing in it. And to know that the only options were to defuse it or get the hell away before it blew.

There was a lot to be said for a strategic retreat. With that in mind, Laramie strode down the dirt track leading away from the cabin with Sammi Jo hot on his heels.

He breathed in the treasured peace of the Guadalupe Mountains, letting it seep into his skin. Chinquapin oaks ranged a few yards back from the path; Mexican orange bushes and skunkbushes dotted the landscape. A red-tailed hawk circled overhead as if welcoming him home.

It would have been perfect.

Would have being the operative phrase.

He glanced at the woman by his side, impressed that she'd kept up so easily. He'd have figured those long legs of hers would have trouble hiking in high heels.

How long were those legs? he wondered. Her dress

hugged her hips, but it was hard to tell under all that white fluff flowing to her knees. The shiny fabric shoes were toast, he noted. Covered in dust, the pointed toes were fraying fast. Probably not too many brides wore them to hike through the hills. Leave it to Sammi to be different.

"Do you do that a lot?" she asked as if realizing his temper had faded.

"Walk?" His usual gentlemanly nature kicking in, he adjusted his stride to match hers. "Pretty much every day."

"Ha. I meant do you kiss women a lot?" She slid him a sideways gaze, her lips pursed in consideration. "I've heard you do, but you know how gossip is. A puff of air is a force-four tornado by the time it gets through the gossip chain."

Wasn't that the truth? It'd been one of many reasons Laramie had been happy to leave Jerrick. Little had he known that he'd be trading small-town gossip for military gossip. And like everything the military did, they were a gossiping machine, so organized that some guys said that each piece of gossip was spread with a salute. Just to make it official.

When they reached the fork in the path, he waited for her gesture before angling left. She must have parked on the road next to the hiking trail instead of the one leading toward the canyon. Only a half mile to go before he could breathe his peaceful air all by himself.

"Well?"

Shifting his eyes from the piñon pine in the distance where the road ran past, Laramie simply arched his brow.

"How many women *have* you kissed?" Sounding some-where between frustrated and fascinated, Sammi frowned. "Hundreds? Thousands?"

Laramie's lips twitched.

"A gentleman doesn't brag." Nor did he keep count.

Not when counting would take on the proportions of a part-time job.

Figuring this topic wasn't doing either of them any good, Laramie stepped up his pace until they came to the clearing by the highway.

"Well, do you just kiss women for the hell of it?" she asked, the frustration overcoming fascination as her words got tighter. "Do you have a weekly quota or something?"

"Sugar, I sometimes spend a month at a time in a submarine or a cave. A weekly quota wouldn't be doable."

"Monthly? Yearly?" she snapped, taking the hand Laramie held out to help her step over the downed log blocking the road. "I'd just like to know where I fit into all of that."

She didn't.

He wouldn't let her.

"I take it that's yours," he said instead of answering. He frowned at the late model Chevy truck tucked between two scrub bushes.

"It's the inn's," Sammi said, gesturing as they came around to where Barclay's name was plastered over the door. "I just drive it."

"Your fiancé owns some fancy-ass dealership, doesn't he?" Hadn't his uncle mentioned that at some point? "What do you drive? A Jag? Mercedes?"

"I drive this." Sammi patted the truck's red fender.

Laramie frowned. Between Barclay's dealership and her working for the richest man in town, she should be rolling in fancy cars, fancy clothes and fancy every-damned-thing.

Before he could ask, Sammi slid her hand down the top of her dress, two fingers slipping inside that lush cleavage. Laramie tipped his hat back a little to get a better look, just in case she needed help or anything.

His fingers itched to dive in there, to slide around that warm, soft skin. To dip deeper until he found her nipple and find out how sensitive it was. To see what sound she'd make when he rubbed it.

Damn, he was getting hard again.

Laramie forced his gaze away from her chest, focusing instead on the cute expression of concentration on her face. She flashed a triumphant smile as she pulled a key out of her top.

"I was afraid I'd lose it if I carried it," she said with a laugh. "I debated hiding it under a rock or something, then realized this dress is so tight, nothing is moving in there."

Damn. Was she really that innocent?

Head tilted, he studied Sammi's face as she unlocked the door and realized that yeah, she really was. He needed to remember that.

"Now what do we do?" she asked, hopping into the driver's seat. She pulled her cell phone out of the cubby in the dash and handed it to him before shifting so that she was angled toward him. Her dress didn't make the shift as easily, the fabric facing forward as her torso faced him. Laramie waited, but nothing interesting popped out. Was she glued in there?

Probably for the best, he acknowledged as his gaze climbed from the fullness of her lace-covered breasts, up the gold silk of chest and long slender throat. Her sharp chin and that full upper lip gave him pause for a moment before Laramie finally met Sammi's eyes.

"We don't do anything. You go home. Do whatever it is you usually do. I'll deal with this." He looked around the dirt road, brush and trees obscuring them from anyone's view. "I'll be in touch."

"What? No way." She reached out to grab his arm before Laramie could move away from the door. "I'm helping find Sterling."

"No." Ignoring the odd comfort her touch gave him,

Laramie shook his head. "You already have an assignment. Make like everything is normal. I'll do the searching."

"I'm not sitting on my butt while my fiancé is in danger." Sammi swung her legs out of the truck, as if to jump down. Laramie stepped forward, blocking her before she could.

"If you want to find Sterling yourself, go ahead. If you want my help, we do it my way." He waited a beat, until the stubborn frustration faded from her face. "You go back to town, you play like things are just fine and you don't contact me."

"Then how do I know what's going on?" Her tut-tutting eye roll clued him in that she had a very different vision of how this was going to go than he did.

"I'm going to tap a few friends, call in a few favors. I'll contact you as soon as I know something. You stay in town. Don't come up here, don't try to contact me, don't even think about mentioning that you saw me." Before she could voice the protest he saw in her eyes, Laramie shifted into command mode. Voice brisk, eyes direct, words strong. "You'll jeopardize your engagement if anyone knows you've been in contact with me."

"That's ridiculous."

Laramie waited a beat.

"So how'd you know I was in town?"

"The gossip chain was rattling, of course. Everyone's talking about the legend of Laramie." She wriggled her brows. "Did you know some of the guys want to erect a statue in your honor at Make Out Peak? Erect being the key word, by the way."

His point made, he simply waited.

After a second, Sammi frowned and shook her head.

"Just because every woman in town wants to ride you like a show horse doesn't mean they'd think I do, too."

Sure they wouldn't.

Sammi gave an irritated sniff, crossed her arms over her breasts in a way that made Laramie want to promise that she'd have the ride of her life.

"Is this some macho SEAL attempt to protect me?"

Hell, no. Laramie automatically shied away from the idea of protecting a single person. He was trained to protect his country, he was conditioned to protect his team. Every hostage extraction, every assignment to aid foreign operatives, every single mission undertaken was done for the simple reason that it was for the good of the country.

He could do that.

He did do that—and he was damned good at it.

But a single person?

Nope. Not happening. Laramie gently turned Sammi toward the steering wheel again, then once her legs were clear, shut the truck door.

He gave her a modified salute with her cell phone, then nodded toward the road.

"I'll be in touch."

6

THERE HAD BEEN many times in her life that Sammi Jo thought she'd gotten a bum deal when it came to life's little blessings.

Her early years as a frizzy-headed carrottop, when she'd wished for fine, straight blond hair.

Grade school, spent struggling with dyslexia while all she'd wanted to do was to lose herself in a book.

Hoping to make a living doing something creative, only to be told her art style was too mundane and not worth pursuing.

And, of course, any and all thoughts of her mother.

But her combined disappointment over all of those missed blessings was nothing compared to how she felt right now.

As Sammi tried to clean up the mess left in her office, she couldn't shake the miserable feeling that her marriage plans were doomed. She righted the desk chair. Every minute she spent searching for the missing wheel a reminder that her fiancé was missing, too.

Kneeling on the floor, she gathered the papers that'd been thrown this way and that—she assumed during his struggle. Panicking wouldn't help, she told herself as she tried to press wrinkles out of a few invoices. But the simple white clock on the wall mocked her with every tick of its tock, reminding her that it'd been eighteen hours since she'd driven away from Laramie and she hadn't heard a word. She didn't know what she'd expected, but it wasn't silence.

She rose, setting the stack of papers on the desk under a book in the hopes of flattening them again. Needing to keep busy, desperate for something to take her mind from jumping from panicked scenario to frantic worry, she grabbed the box of booking software that Mr. Barclay wanted installed.

Twenty minutes later, her mind was definitely distracted but her stress level was even higher.

It'd taken her two tries to even get it to turn on and even then, it'd taken forever to boot up.

Now, for the fifth time, her screen flashed an error message as she tried to install the program. Sammi jabbed the enter button again. And again. And again.

The monitor went black. A white line intersected the screen for a brief second before the error message flashed again.

Stupid freaking computer.

Sammi smacked the heel of her hand against her computer monitor and growled.

"Sammi Jo. What do you think you're doing? That's an expensive piece of equipment."

Biting back a yelp, Sammi jumped to her feet, the chair skidding one way while its broken wheel shot under her desk.

Mr. Barclay scowled at her from the doorway. A bull of a man, he didn't fit in the cramped quarters of the inn's office. Which was why he usually called Sammi to his.

"You know that I expect my people to show proper respect." He huffed, so that with his silvery mane of hair he sounded like a grumpy lion. "You're supposed to set an example, Sammi Jo. Now more than ever. Do you want your staff to think that you're taking advantage of your engagement?"

"No, of course not." Sammi fought the urge to hunch her shoulders, but did surreptitiously tug at the waistband of the sundress she'd worn with her bridal shower in mind.

"I've left numerous messages that you've neglected to return." His bushy brows drew together as he peered around. Sammi held her breath. Had she cleaned up all evidence of Sterling's abduction? Her gaze shot through the room like a well-aimed pinball. It looked normal, but she couldn't relax.

"I prefer not to have to track you down, Sammi. I dislike leaving my office during business hours," Mr. Barclay continued, his eyes now resting on the miserable excuse of a computer.

She had to curl her fingers together to keep from pointing to the landline right there on the corner of her desk. But what if there was something wrong with it? She resisted the urge to grab the receiver and check for herself. Was that why she hadn't heard from Laramie? He'd said he'd have her cell phone back to her today. Had something happened?

It wasn't until the tiny black spots started dancing in front of her eyes that Sammi realized she wasn't breathing.

Whoosh. Deep breath in, deep breath out. She had to blink a few times to clear the dots, but soon Mr. Barclay came back into focus. As if etched from white oak, his features were strong and decisive underneath his full head of silver hair.

She finally managed a stiff smile.

"I'm sorry you weren't able to reach my cell phone.

I've been having some technical difficulties. What was it you needed?"

"I've gone over your budget for this new wedding project and made a few adjustments." Still standing in the doorway, he held out a file folder.

Her wedding? Was she even going to have one?

Breathing through the panic, she focused on Laramie's promise. He said he'd find Sterling. He told her to act normal, to keep her head and that everything would be fine.

If she expected him to do his part, the least she could do was hers.

Sammi forced herself to focus. Okay. The wedding. Brow drawn, she walked over to take the file.

A quick glance was all it took to realize he was referring to Weddings at the Barclay Inn. Not her own wedding. Breathing a little easier, Sammi flipped open the folder and pursed her lips.

"These are significant cuts," she noted absently, flipping through the top few pages.

"Do you have an issue with them?" he barked.

"I don't know until I read them," Sammi said with a smile and a shrug. Unlike Sterling, she wasn't put off by the older man's gruff demeanor. After all, it was his challenging personality in part that made her continually strive to be better at her job. "I'm sorry you had to come over just for this."

"That, and to find out if you've seen that boy of mine."

Sammi's stomach constricted as he shot a beetle-browed look around the office as if Sterling might be hiding in the corner.

"No. I haven't seen Sterling since yesterday," she said, hoping that honesty would carry the rest of the lies. Her cheeks on fire, Sammi forced herself to channel the best liar she knew, her mother. "But he did say he had a new project that was taking him out of town for a few days. He's really excited about it. I think this might be a big opportunity. Like, huge, big."

Sammi held her arms out as wide as she could, her smile so broad it hurt her face.

"Well. Hmm." As if surprised by her enthusiasm, Mr. Barclay nodded. "That's good. Good to know."

She was so impressed with her performance that when she dropped her hands, Sammi surreptitiously slid one down her side to make sure she was still wearing her underwear. Yep, still there.

Whew. One lying performance did not her mother make.

"Still, Sterling should have had the courtesy to call me directly. I know what you're going to say. He was excited." Waving away his son's make-believe enthusiasm as if it didn't matter, Mr. Barclay shook his head. "A man runs his business, he doesn't let his business run him. To do otherwise shows poor management skills. I blame that partner of his. What was the boy thinking, bringing a complete stranger like Carl Dillard into the business without consulting me? The man is a hustler. Only interested in get-rich-quick schemes."

As Mr. Barclay launched into his familiar rant about how he wouldn't be taken advantage of, not even by his son, Sammi could only grimace. Because while she didn't think that Sterling was a poor businessman, she did agree that Carl wasn't a good partner. He did more traveling than working, for one thing. And there was something about him that reminded Sammi of the third, eighth and ninth *uncle* her mother had brought home.

"Well, enough of that." He harrumphed a little before smiling. "Since Sterling didn't have the courtesy to let me know he'd miss lunch, you can come with me instead."

"I really wish I could, but I'm supposed to be at a bridal

shower soon and wanted to get this software installed," she said, frowning at the clock. "I can meet you for dinner instead, if you'd like?"

"No, of course not." His refusal didn't surprise her, but it did hurt just a little. Mr. Barclay saw lunch as business, and dinner as personal, but she'd have thought by marrying his son she'd have merited a meal after 4:00 p.m. Sammi blinked at the tears burning her eyes and pressed her lips tight to keep her smile in place.

Not that he was looking.

"A number of the guests attending your bridal events are quite influential. Don't forget that you're a representative of the Barclay empire, Sammi Jo," he said as he left the room. "Behave appropriately."

"SAMMI JO, HAVE YOU and Sterling decided when you want the children to arrive?"

What children? Sammi frowned into her china teacup as she realized they meant *her* having children. Did she want to have children? Wasn't that something she should have thought about before her lingerie bridal shower?

Sammi swapped out her teacup for a glass of rum-spiked punch.

"And how many do you want? Sterling must at least be planning for a boy, of course, to carry on the family name."

"I'm sure Sterling would love that," Sammi said, not sure at all. The thought had her draining her punch.

And hoping Mr. Barclay didn't hear about her drinking. She'd started with tea, a nice orange pekoe. But sitting in the private dining room of Martella's, the fanciest restaurant in town, with her bridesmaids, a handful of friends and twenty women she barely knew, seemed to require a drink or four. She'd had her first during present time, needing something to help her get through the commentary that came with each piece of lingerie she'd unwrapped. But now kids?

Oh, boy.

She looked around for more punch.

"So what do you think?" Clara leaned over the back of Sammi's flower-bedecked chair to show her the bouquet she'd made of the gift ribbons. Streamers of silver satin flowed to the floor from a small mountain of glittering apricot-colored bows. "I think mine will win the contest."

What contest? Had she missed something? Sammi glanced around the restaurant's private room. Rich mahogany and brocade were offset by bell-shaped flower arrangements. Silver tea services were placed within arm's reach of every place setting, and trays of tiny sandwiches, delicate cookies and glossy tarts sat next to each plate. The guests themselves were like a flower garden, in their colorful summer dresses and best shoes.

But Sammi didn't see anything that looked like a contest.

"Not fair," Mia declared before she could ask. "You made everyone wrap the gifts in the bridal colors. How do the rest of us stand a chance at our shower bouquets being chosen as the one she uses at the rehearsal?"

There was a contest for that?

Who had to choose the winner? Not her, right?

Sammi glanced at the ribbons again and frowned. Since Mrs. Ross had changed her colors, deeming the bridesmaids' dresses enough purple, she could pick. She'd end up overruling Sammi's choice, anyway.

"Hmm, clever of me, right?" Clara laughed, then looked around the table, gauging everyone's plate. "Now that we've had tea and opened gifts, shall we have cake?"

Clara toted her prize-winning bouquet over to the cake

table. Sammi started to rise to help with dessert, but the slew of protests stopped her.

"You're the guest of honor," Amy reminded her, folding a sheer red peignoir set and placing it on top of a black satin merry widow. "You just sit here and enjoy being pampered."

With that and a quick pat to Sammi's shoulder she went back to packing the gifts.

"This is a great lingerie suitcase," the brunette said as she kept piling silk after lace after satin into it. "And look at these panties. Who gave Sammi these again?"

Amy held up a black thong with the words *Do Me* embroidered in red. Sammi grabbed the blue pair with *Insert Here* on them before Amy could wave those, too.

Since most of the women were still talking and eating, Amy consulted the notepad where Clara had listed all of the gifts and givers. Sammi wondered at the proper way to word a thank-you note for pornographic underwear.

She couldn't imagine Sterling's reaction. Would he laugh?

Laramie would. Sammi could just see his expression, those light eyes crinkling at the corners and that smile of his taking on a wicked edge. He'd probably say something about needing to give the gift a test run in order to offer a proper thanks. Sammi's fingers slid along the smooth satin fabric, imagining Laramie doing the same. His fingers were so long, and she'd bet there was talent in every inch. Would he be gentle when he touched? Would he go slow and soft, teasing every drop of pleasure from the touch? Or would he take? Intense and just a little rough with passionate demand.

Whew. She puffed out a breath. It was getting hot in here.

"Excuse me," she murmured, pushing away from the

table. She needed air. It took her five minutes to make her way through the well-wishers. Despite the urge to head for the door, she settled for the restroom.

She was splashing cold water on her wrists when Blythe walked in.

"What's wrong?"

"Too many rum punches," Sammi said, trying to smile but settling on a half shrug. "And it's a little overwhelming."

"Mmm," Blythe murmured, her eyes on Sammi's face as she held out a towel. "How long have we known each other?"

Uh oh.

Not that question.

She could never hold out against that question.

"We've known each other for over twenty years, haven't we?" Blythe answered when Sammi didn't. "Of course, it doesn't take knowing you since we were four and crashed our bikes so our training wheels got stuck together. All it takes is simple observation to see that something's wrong."

Sammi bit her lip, trying not to cry.

"Are you having second thoughts about marrying Sterling?"

Second, third and fourth ones, too. But she couldn't do anything about them when the man was gone, held captive God knows where. Sammi's bottom lip trembled as she tried to breathe past the knot in her chest. She stared at her hands, unable to look at her own reflection or meet Blythe's eyes.

"Sammi... No, wait." Despite her high heels, Blythe crouched down to peek and make sure the bathroom stall was empty, then gave Sammi her most serious look. Quite a feat for a woman wearing purple chiffon with red polka dots and green heels. "You don't have to go through with it, you know."

"Probably not the proper thing to say at a bridal shower," Sammi joked with a watery laugh. "I mean, they're already cutting the cake."

"To hell with the cake. Are you happy? Not do you think you should be happy," she interrupted before Sammi could respond. "Not are you satisfied making other people happy. This is just about you right now. Are *you* happy?"

She'd been happy when Laramie kissed her. But she knew that didn't count.

"No." Sammi shook her head as the misery of everything—Sterling's disappearance, her fears, all the doubts and second thoughts—took hold. "But—"

"No but," Blythe interrupted, her pixie face folding into a scowl. "This is the rest of your life we're talking about, Sammi Jo. You don't base the rest of your life on a *but*. You base it on happy."

"We can't be happy all the time," Sammi pointed out. More for something to do than because it needed it, she took a comb from her purse to slide through her hair. Since it was easier to ignore Blythe's words if she didn't look directly at her, Sammi focused on her own image as she tidied her russet waves.

"No. But there are times that we should have so much happy that we're overflowing. The weeks leading up to promising to spend the rest of your life with someone should be one of those times." Blythe grimaced as if she knew her words weren't going to be welcome, but she couldn't hold them back any longer. "Sammi, I haven't seen you look happy—truly happy—in the last six months. Ever since you got engaged to Sterling. Now, maybe that's just the times I'm seeing. Maybe you're doing giant cartwheels of happiness a lot of the time and I'm not around to see them."

"You know I can't do a cartwheel," Sammi said, trying to joke it off as she exchanged the comb for her powder compact. "But you're right. I have been stressed lately. This wedding stuff is crazy, it really is."

"So that's it? The wedding has you stressed out," Blythe repeated, her words as stiff as her posture.

"You've met Mrs. Ross. The woman is a nightmare. She's taken over everything, changed all of my ideas, so it's as if it's not even my wedding. Even this," she waved her hand toward the door to indicate the party in the other room, "isn't me. I had to be introduced to half those women out there. Next thing I know, they're talking about my underwear and advising me on preschools. They expect me to serve on committees and to lunch at the country club. It's as if I'm supposed to turn into this other person and I don't even know if I like her."

As the words poured out, Sammi realized that they were more than a smokescreen to keep from telling Blythe about Sterling. They were 100 percent true.

"You have friends in there, too," Blythe reminded her in a soft voice, rubbing her hand over Sammi's arm. "Friends who accept you just the way you are."

She only gave Sammi enough time to nod before continuing.

"But the rest of them, that's the world you're marrying, Sammi Jo. And it's one thing to take on all of those changes, to face all of those expectations and demands, if you have love and a happy relationship to balance it out."

Sammi knew that was more of a question than a statement. A question that Blythe wanted an answer to. Maybe it was all the rum swimming through her head, but it didn't require a lot of thinking or soul searching to figure out. And how sad was that?

"I thought having friendship, common goals and respect would be enough," Sammi said quietly as she faced Blythe with a sigh. "It still might be. But I have to talk with Sterling and I can't do that until he's back."

"Okay." Blythe nodded, the move setting her glittering red earrings to spinning. She held out her arms, like a rainbow of friendship always there to brighten Sammi's day. When Sammi leaned in for a quick hug, Blythe whispered. "I'll be here, whatever happens. And it'll be fine. We'll make sure of it."

Unable to pretend at just that second, Sammi laid her forehead against Blythe's and closed her eyes. "Thanks," she whispered.

Taking a deep breath, she hugged Blythe tight, then stepped back.

"I'll start bawling in a minute," she said with a trembling smile.

"You and me both." While Sammi took deep yoga breaths and repaired her makeup again, Blythe fanned her eyes with her fingers to dry them. "Okay, I'm going to go out and tell them you had a phone call. Maybe an emergency at the inn. You take your time in here, or better yet take a walk outside. Clear your head until you can come back in and say a friendly goodbye. Then we'll head back to your place and finish getting drunk and talk this all through."

Sammi wanted to. Oh, how she wanted to tell Blythe everything. About Sterling's kidnapping, his cheating. About Laramie's kiss and how hot and crazy he made Sammi feel with just one look.

But she couldn't.

The second she confessed all of that, Sammi was afraid

of everything else that would spill from her lips. Besides, she couldn't risk Sterling's safety by saying anything.

Lips reslicked, she gave Blythe a grateful smile.

"I'm gonna take you up on that first part and clear my head. But the drunk confessions will have to wait a few days." Before Blythe could voice the protest that went with her frown, Sammi took her head. "I will, as soon as I can, though. Just not yet."

Blythe looked as if she was going to pout. Instead, though, she gave Sammi a finger wag.

"You promise?"

"I promise."

"Then go. Skip on out of here for a little while. I've got you covered."

Not sure if it was guilt or excitement that was making her dizzy, Sammi stepped out first. Her stomach contorted when she glanced toward the private room where a handful of friends and a whole lot of strangers were celebrating her upcoming marriage. Oh yeah, it was guilt.

"Go," Blythe urged with a shoulder bump.

So Sammi went.

Trying to ignore the guilt tapping its way up and down her spine, Sammi hurried from the room. In case anyone was watching, she headed for the front of the restaurant. After a quick hello to the owner and a glance over her shoulder, she slipped out the side door.

The warm evening air spun through her, making her feel as if just breathing was doubling her blood alcohol content. Sammi made her way on slightly unsteady steps toward the alley between the restaurant and Barclay bank.

As she rounded the building, a tall form stepped from the shadows. She didn't need to see the face beneath the white Stetson to know it was Laramie. Even shrouded in the dark, that body was unmistakable.

"There you are," she said with a breathless laugh as she fell into Laramie's chest. She wrapped her arms around his waist to steady herself, then left them there because, mmm yeah, it felt good. "I've been waiting forever."

"Forever, is it?" Laramie grasped her hips, his fingers hard and hot through the soft cotton of her skirt as he gently moved her back a few inches. "I suppose that is a long time to go without your phone."

But she hadn't been waiting for her phone. She'd been waiting for him.

Not because she was lusting after his body, she assured herself, thankful for the alcohol-laced fruit-juice buzz that drowned out her mind's mocking laugh. She was so happy to see him because he was the only one who understood what she was going through. The only one who she didn't have to pretend with.

Heat stirred low in her belly as she stared into his shadowed features. His hands still gripped her hips, making her want to squirm closer. To wrap her legs around the hard length of his and ride him like a racehorse until he took her over the finish line and relieved the hot, aching pressure building inside of her.

Sammi blew out a long, slow breath, wishing she could release the tension as easily.

Looked like she needed to pretend a little after all. With that in mind, she tried to pull her thoughts together. But between the alcohol swirling through her mind and the temptation just inches away, it wasn't easy. He was probably here for something besides bringing her cell phone and getting her all hot and bothered.

Sammi frowned, trying to focus. Finally it clicked.

"Sterling." Guilt and worry rushed through her so fast, Sammi felt dizzy. Or maybe that was the fruit juice. "Do you have news about Sterling?"

"Not really."

Her stomach knotted so tight she was afraid she'd be sick. Whether sensing her distress or worried she'd hurl on his boots, Laramie tightened his grip.

"I contacted a friend who's a communications wizard. He tracked the call as far as the cell tower it used. It's local, putting him in the range vicinity. Another buddy is a genius with information. He sent me details on Barclay's business, his partner, his finances. I put a copy in your truck, tucked under the driver's seat. It'd help if you go through them, too. Maybe something'll pop for you." Laramie shrugged at Sammi's expression. "You want me to find him? I have to know where to look."

"I guess so," she said slowly, wishing they didn't have to invade Sterling's privacy. He was so fussy about his personal space, and here she and Laramie were, poking all through it.

Laramie folded one hand over hers, lifting them to his lips. His shadowed eyes met hers over their joined hands, his breath warming her as he pulled her a little closer.

And just like that, she felt better. It was as if he had flipped a switch, instantly turning her worry into hot, needy lust.

"You okay?"

No. She was melting into a gooey puddle of desire.

"I'm good. I'm really, really good." Her gaze drifting to his mouth; she wet her lips and wondered… How many ways could he kiss? She'd liked the one she'd tried—if hot-dream-inspired desire qualified as like.

Sammi sighed, her body going soft as she imagined.

Tucking his free hand under her chin, Laramie leaned back to inspect her face. His sober expression shifted into a wicked smile.

"Okay, is it? Been drinking, sugar?"

"Just juice."

Wanting so much to try another kiss, Sammi moved even closer until her legs brushed his. Her thighs trembled. Their joined hands prevented full body contact, but if she could get turned on with just a knee knock? Who knew what would happen with the next kiss.

"That's all? Juice?" he asked absently, the words seeming to come from a long way away. He released her hands before sliding both of his into her hair. Tilting her head back a little, he gave her a long, intense stare that made Sammi's entire body hot. Her nipples puckered tight and her thighs trembled as he held her gaze captive, slowly lowering his head until his mouth brushed over hers.

Oh.

Sammi might have moaned that against his lips or the sound might have reverberated through her head, she didn't know. Because all she could think was *ohhhh*.

His tongue swept into her mouth with teasing little forays, each thrust making Sammi wetter, making her nether lips tremble with need. She grabbed his arms. This time she did moan aloud as her hands skimmed under the sleeves of his soft cotton T, rubbing the hard flesh. He was so big. So strong. Her palms smoothed over the rounded concrete of his biceps, fingers skimming then soothing before starting all over again.

Need pounded through her, the beat quickening with each second. Soon, her fingers were digging into his biceps, her hips pressing desperately against his.

More. All she could think now was that she wanted more.

She tried to shift even closer, but the hands gripping her hair kept their upper bodies apart. Frustration added an edge to the need, deepening the urgency. Heat curled low in her belly, ready to explode with just the right touch.

Please, she thought. Touch her right.

As if sensing how close she was, Laramie slowly pulled his mouth from hers. She felt him take a deep breath, but his eyes were steady and his expression mild.

A frown worked its way through Sammi's heady need. Why wasn't he affected? She wanted him as excited as he'd made her. She wanted, so, *so* wanted, to push him to the edge of an orgasm with just one kiss.

"There's an awful lot of rum in your juice, Sammi. You might want to go back in there and switch to water." His words were low and a little amused.

Sammi felt a pout coming on.

"I don't want to go back in there. They are comparing underwear and debating the best flavor of body oil."

Aha. Triumph surged through her at the look on his face.

Desire. She might not be as up on all things sexual, but Sammi recognized lusty desire when it was aimed her way. Fueled by the fruit-juice-laced rum, she called up every teasing move she'd ever seen or read.

She tilted her chin down just a little and gave him a beseeching look through the sweep of her lashes. She tiptoed her fingers up his warm chest, her nails scraping his nipples as she passed. His eyes narrowed, but otherwise Laramie didn't react.

Undeterred, Sammi skimmed her palms along the sides of his neck, then cupped them over his cheeks.

Her eyes locked on his, she pressed closer so her breasts were crushed against his chest. The feel was so intense, so powerful that she couldn't stop her small moan of pleasure.

"They are debating what type of panties get a guy hotter," she whispered, her mouth close to his. "Some of them say French cut, others insist on thongs. A handful swear by the power of going bare."

She waited a beat, watching those golden hazel eyes narrow.

"What's your favorite, Laramie?" She rubbed her lips against his, then smiled. "What turns you on?"

Before she realized his intention, Laramie grabbed her arms and spun her around so she was trapped between the brick wall and his body.

Triumph flashed, fast and giddy.

Then his mouth crushed hers. As his tongue thrust, Sammi Jo's last thought was that she was way, way out of her league. And then sensation took over. Desire, so hot and needy, grew with each sweep of his tongue. She didn't realize he'd slid his hand down her hip until she felt the warmth of his hand against the lace of her panties and realized he'd pulled her skirt up.

She trembled, gripping his shoulders to keep from simply melting into a puddle of lust all over his feet.

His fingers slid along the hem of her panties—a thong if he was checking. Pleasure coiled. He skimmed his thumb over her mound, back and forth. As she sank into the pleasure of that, his fingers drummed a beat between her thighs, tapping gently on her swollen, aching lips.

Sammi gasped as her body contracted. Laramie sucked her tongue into his mouth, his teeth scraping as he tapped faster.

She exploded, riding on a wave of a million tiny pieces of pleasure so intense she didn't think she'd ever come down.

"Oh, God," she moaned, her head falling back against the bricks with a soft thud. Her body vibrating with pleasure, Sammi didn't try to think. She didn't bother with guilt and ignored every attempt worry made to burst her bubble.

Nope, she determined, trying to draw in a breath. Nothing was getting in the way of her enjoying every blessed second of her first semipublic, against-the-wall orgasm.

LARAMIE WAS IN TROUBLE. Serious, mind-blowing trouble.

He'd gotten a lot of women off in his time—so many that he'd developed quite a reputation for it. He'd even driven a few—okay, more than a few, but who was counting—to fully dressed, screaming orgasms.

But Laramie had never been this close to losing it himself. To wanting to drop his pants and drive into the hot, wet welcome of a woman's trembling body. If it'd been any other woman, he'd have given in to the urge.

But Sammi Jo was different.

In so many ways.

Only one of which was that she trusted him. She believed in him to protect her.

So, as difficult as it was, Laramie took a deep breath and called up his reserve control—a rare necessity since his front lines almost never failed. But they were failing now, big time.

"I've got to go."

"Do you have to? I want to come." Sammi rubbed her thumb over his lower lip, her smile taking on a wicked edge. "Again."

"Again, huh?" His mouth was halfway to hers, before he remembered that he wasn't going to do this.

The woman was actually making him forget his resolve. Not sure he could hold out against her needs and his own body's demands, Laramie went on the offensive.

"Does your fiancé know this about you?" he asked with a deceptively easy smile as he put two feet of distance between himself and the tempting warmth of her curvaceous body.

Sammi blinked, either at the question or at the mention

of Sterling. A small trickle of guilt worked its way down Laramie's spine at the look on her face. He'd been the one taking advantage of an inebriated woman. But before he could apologize, Sammi gave a slow shrug. The move sent the strap of her dress sliding lower, the fabric of her dress an erotic showcase to those still-pouting nipples.

Laramie's apology froze in his throat.

"I really don't think he does know," Sammi mused, shaking her head. "He's not really into this stuff."

Laramie blinked.

What had they been talking about?

"Beg pardon?"

"This." Sammi twirled her finger between their bodies. "You know, the physical stuff."

He shook his head, sure he was misreading her words.

"We're more about friendly support," she explained, leaning her head back against the wall as if standing upright was too much effort. "You know. We're there for each other. We support the other's dreams and give them a sounding board for their frustrations."

Laramie's frown deepened the longer he listened to Sammi's description of her relationship with the man she planned to spend the rest of her life with.

Where was the fun?

The passion?

Hell, where was the sex?

By the time she got to long walks and the same taste in sports, Laramie was ready to suggest she skip marriage and just get herself a dog.

It sounded like that's what she wanted, and a dog would be more loyal—and probably better looking—than Barclay.

"So all in all, I doubt he knows this about me," Sammi

concluded with a tipsy smile. "Unless he's imagined it. Can guys tell that kind of thing?"

His head reeling, Laramie gave in to the urge to pinch the bridge of his nose, hoping it'd help ground him.

Nope. He was still baffled.

"Can guys tell what kind of thing?" he finally asked, not sure he should hear the answer but not willing to walk away when she was sharing it.

"Can guys tell when a woman wants sex? I mean, really wants it?" Her eyes widened, the thick lashes a vivid contrast to her milky-white skin. "Do they know what kind of things a woman likes? I mean, can you look at me and know what turns me on?"

She was trying to kill him.

That was the only explanation he could think of for a question like that.

Because, damn it all to hell if she posed one more sexually charged inquiry, he'd either show her the answer in a very up-close and personally pleasurable way. Or he'd drop dead right here in this alley from sexual frustration.

"I've got to go." He set her aside, heading for the street as fast as his protesting erection would let him.

"Do you *really* have to?" Sammi tilted her head to one side, her hair falling in soft waves over her cheek.

Hell, yes he did.

As fast as he could.

"Laramie?"

He stopped at the edge of the alley and looked back.

Sammi's breasts glowed in the moonlight, full and inviting above the lace trim of her dress. His gaze traced her body wrapped so softly in that pale green fabric, stopping just below her knees. She was soft there, he knew. Soft and sensitive.

His head filled with the memory of her wrapping one

of those legs around his hip, her hot core pressed against his hand while he held her knee in the other.

The woman was dangerous.

And damned if he didn't live for danger. Laramie lifted his gaze to hers.

"Where are you going?" She wet her lips, the damp glistening invitingly.

She'd asked if he could tell what a woman wanted and Laramie had to admit that it was a skill he'd been born with. So he knew all he'd have to do was hold out his hand and she'd go with him.

Damn his morals. Laramie's fists closed tight against the frustration.

"I'm going to find your damned fiancé."

Before he did something so unbelievably stupid he could never recover from it.

Like actually fall in love.

7

LARAMIE HAD SERVED in numerous dangerous missions. With each one he knew it could easily be his last. He accepted that fact with good grace and an easy faith in his skills, his team and the reality that sooner or later those might not be enough.

As he drove down the highway, Tim McGraw blaring from the dash and hot wind blowing through the open windows, he had to admit that this sense of desperate urgency he was feeling was brand-new and just about as welcome as a case of hives. He was torn between figuring Barclay deserved whatever mess he'd landed in and wanting to find the guy and put an end to all contact with Sammi Jo.

The woman was playing havoc on his peace of mind.

Another first.

He was all for giving a lady his complete focus when he was with her. But he'd always been an *out of sight, out of mind* kind of guy.

He'd never lain in bed at night, unable to sleep because his thoughts were filled with a woman. He'd never struggled with need as his mind relived the sound of her orgasm with more pleasure than if it'd been his own. A fact he'd proved when frustration had finally forced him to take matters into his own hands—so to speak.

That didn't mean he was feeling anything special for her. He didn't have any sort of conflict about finding her another man, one she'd spend her life with. The man she'd spend her nights with. That she'd share her body with.

Laramie's teeth snapped together.

Nope. No big deal.

Unwilling to admit—even to himself—just how much bullshit he was shoveling over himself, Laramie focused on the matter at hand.

Typically before a mission, the team was briefed with the most current intel so they went into the situation fully armed. Laramie didn't have a team backing him and he was armed with only his wits. But he did know where to go for the best intel.

He pulled into the gravel lot a few yards off the highway, parking between a truck with a lift kit on steroids and a rusty old heap with a missing bumper.

There was no shortage of bars in Jerrick and its surroundings, with the Wild Bronco one the seedier choice. Most people in these parts knew it for its hot wings, weak beer and wicked bar fights, but it was as much a gossip hub as Curl Up and Dye in town.

Perfect for Laramie's needs.

As he sauntered into the Wild Bronco, a part of him expected to hear Buck Parsons yell from behind the bar for him to get the hell out like he had so many times before. But all that greeted him was the sound of voices bouncing off the walls in counterpoint to the ricochet of pool balls and the music twanging from the jukebox.

He followed the short hallway with its walls studded with trophies, most with jackets hanging from their antlers, and stopped at the main room to look around.

His gaze landed on the bartender and Laramie's lips twitched. Not everything was smaller.

In a sweat-stained cap and a checked shirt missing one of its mother-of-pearl snaps, the guy manning the taps was almost as wide as he was tall.

Dozens of memories flashed through his mind. The times Buck had brought his father home because the old man was too wasted to drive. How many mornings had he come by searching for his dad, only to find that he'd chosen to pass out on the bar instead of catching a ride home? Those mornings, Buck had scrambled him an egg and talked to him about the older man's years in the Navy. The last time he'd seen Buck was at Cole Laramie's funeral; Buck's beady eyes had been wet with tears.

Laramie sauntered toward the rough-hewn bar. He was about a foot away when Buck glanced over. Eyes bulging in his pale face, the burly mountain of a man gaped as if he'd seen a ghost.

Laramie swung a leg over the bar stool and pushed his hat farther back from his face and gave a respectful nod.

"Sonofabitch." His eyes still bugging a little, Buck gave a slow shake of his head. "Boy, you are the spittin' image of your daddy."

Only in looks, he hoped.

But Laramie simply smiled.

"Hey there, Buck. How's it going?"

"Sonofabitch," Buck repeated, reaching over to slap Laramie on the shoulder. His eyes assessing, the bartender leaned his arms on the bar. "Look at you. I heard you'd been through town."

"Art told you?" Laramie guessed, a little surprised his uncle had mentioned it.

"Art? Hell, no. That ole boy doesn't even come down for supplies now that he's got help on the ranch." Buck shook his head, obviously as baffled by Art's reclusiveness as Laramie figured Art was over Buck's gregariousness. "You're a legend, boy. Everyone talks about it when you come to town. They wonder what you're doing up there in the mountains. What you're doing when away. What they're really wondering is *who* you're doing here or there."

"Not much to wonder about." Laramie said with a shrug. His lips twitched as Buck's expectant look faded into resigned acceptance when nothing more was forthcoming. "I'll have a beer."

"Draft okay?"

"Afraid I'm going to ask for one of those craft beers? You got any bacon-flavored beer back there?"

Laramie craned his neck as if checking behind the bar while Buck gave a gravelly chuckle. Turning to get the beer, the large man shot Laramie a look over his shoulder.

"Bet you could find some in town. Try Barclay's Bar. They cater to the tourists and yahoos with more money than taste."

His body tightening at the opening, Laramie forced himself to let it pass. If he jumped on it now, Buck would have word spread through Jerrick that Laramie was back and looking at the Barclays before Laramie wiped the beer foam from his lip.

Didn't matter if it was explosives, women or information. Timing was everything.

So Laramie turned to rest his elbows on the bar and studied the crowd. Pretty impressive for five in the afternoon. "You're doing good business, I see."

"Well, that there's why." Grinning from one hairy ear to the other, Buck gestured toward the television screen that took most of one entire wall. "We got the biggest TV in town, kid. No better place to watch a game. Baseball, football, soccer, you name it. I got them all right here, on demand."

He waved a slender black remote control.

"You wanna watch something? Usually I charge for special requests, but seeing as you're Cole's boy and back for the first time, I'll make this one on the house."

Having no option except to nod his thanks, Laramie chose a random game from the guide Buck offered. The bartender slapped his hands together, rubbed, then wielded the remote like a master.

"Impressive," Laramie said, surprised to realize he was enjoying himself. He took a healthy swallow of his beer and watched the players take the field while gauging his timing.

"So a lot of the townies get in here?" he asked, referring to the people who lived inside the city limits. He didn't figure Barclay had ever set foot in Buck's. Not ritzy enough for his pansy ass. But people who worked for him might, and they'd be the ones who'd know where he could be.

"A few. We're a little out of the way for most of them. Mostly they go to the meat market out on the highway. Less chance their old ladies will catch them than if they drank in town." Buck rolled his eyes at the idea of anyone giving a damn what their wife or girlfriend thought.

Laramie listened to Buck ramble, waiting for any of the names Genius had provided. Aiden Masters's call sign was apt, given that the guy had not only provided names but detailed dossiers on everyone from Barclay's old man to his tailor.

"Hey there, ain't you Laramie?" Interrupting them, a beefy guy plunked his basket of peanuts on the counter next to Laramie's elbow and gestured for another beer. "Teddy Clemens, man. Sat next to you in Mr. Jones's third grade class. Remember me?"

Third grade. Laramie frowned. Was that the year he and his mom had followed his dad from Texas to Wyoming and then Montana? What'd it been? Two months before Cole Laramie had scored two points shy of winning his saddle bronc competition and took his loss out on his wife before sending them the hell out of his face. Or was third grade the year Laramie had tried to convince his father to take him on the circuit with him by hopping on Old Blue? If he remembered correctly, the bronc had sent him flying over the fence and headfirst into a tree. He could still hear his father's laughter over the ringing that'd sounded in his head.

Laramie studied the ruddy face as the other man cracked a peanut, tossed the nuts high to catch in his mouth while the shells hit the floor.

Nope.

Laramie had a lot of memories. But none of this guy.

But he hadn't been raised by the head good ole boy of the good ole boys' club for nothing. Laramie knew how to play the game.

"Hey there, Teddy. What've you been up to all these years?"

"Running cable for the phone company, man. It pays good, and keeps Barb happy." As if Laramie had expressed an inkling of interest, Teddy reached around to pull a chained leather wallet from his back pocket and started showing off pictures. "That's my Barb. Check her out, Buck. Looking good with that four pointer, ain't she?"

As Buck and Teddy admired the woman and/or the deer, Laramie nursed what was left of his beer and let their conversation roll around him. Just as he was pondering the oddities of life and the uselessness of ever thinking you'd gotten away from the past, Teddy nudged his arm.

"Didn't your mama work for Barclay?"

Yeah, she had. Right up until the old man fired her for taking too many days off to deal with his daddy's funeral. His face set at the memory, Laramie nodded.

"That SOB, he sure ain't improved with age. Repossessed my daddy's farm a few years back." His affable face angling into a sneer, Teddy crushed his next peanut so the dust powdered his belly. "That man is mean as a rattler and twice as ugly."

And there it was.

His opening.

Making a show of leaning back on the stool and crossing one booted foot over the other, Laramie did another quick recon of the room. Two guys bending over the pool table were too close to the jukebox to hear. Buck had his eyes glued to the game on his big screen pride and joy, and the other handful of patrons were drunk.

"What about his son? Did he ever leave town to become the king of the world like he figured he deserved?"

"Sterling?" Teddy laughed, spraying bits of peanut across the bar. "He's too lazy to be king. He's just biding his time until he can dip into daddy's money."

"Not lazy," Buck corrected. "Uppity. That boy thinks he's too good for the likes of us."

"Got himself engaged to Cora Mae's girl. Talk about hot." Leering, Teddy blew on the tips of his fingers.

"Watch your mouth," Buck interrupted, swapping empty bottles for full ones. "Don't be bad mouthin' Sammi Jo. That girl worked hard to get out from under her mama's reputation."

"Hard enough to land herself the son of the richest man in town," Teddy argued, his face settling into stubborn lines. "Sounds an awful lot like Cora Mae to me."

"Deserves better than Barclay, that's for sure," Buck

muttered, whipping a rag out of his belt and rubbing it over the bar. "Cheatin' bastard."

Barclay was cheating on Sammi? Aiden hadn't geniused that out in his research. Laramie's fist clenched tight against the urge to punch something.

"Ain't married yet," Teddy pointed out, gesturing with his beer. "Guy's got a right to do whatever he wants before that ring's shoved on his finger."

"A promise is a promise." Buck gave Laramie a look from under his bushy brows as if daring him to say different.

Nope. Laramie agreed. Promises were sacred. But agreeing would put Teddy on the defensive, so Laramie simply tipped back his beer for another swallow.

Besides, he knew the less he said, the more blanks they'd fill in.

"He's doing Janette Glass. She moved here, what? About three years ago?" He looked to Buck for confirmation. "Waitress at the bar on Second Street."

"I heard tell that he was seeing that widow who owns the dry cleaners."

"My ma heard it from ole Bill who runs the liquor store that Maggie Conner comes in every third Friday of the month to pick up a bottle of that fancy French wine that Barclay likes. Then they have a ron-day-vous at the Red Roof Inn."

"Cheap bastard making her bring the booze," Buck muttered.

While Teddy, Buck and a few others joined in to share the private details of Sterling Barclay's life, Laramie simply gathered the information he needed.

Sammi's fiancé was a cheating snake, they all agreed on that. His business partner Carl was shady enough to give wide berth, but the man must be good for something because business was way better than Sterling was capable of.

But nobody said anything that hinted toward a motivation for kidnapping, nor did they voice a single suspicion over the man's recent absence.

Laramie carefully committed the details to memory. He'd follow up, double—maybe even triple—check before he broke it to Sammi Jo.

Then he'd have to figure out how to tell her that the man she was about to marry was a lying, cheating jerk without using that news as an opportunity to strip her naked and introduce her to pleasures beyond her wildest dreams.

Three hours, a quick march over Devil's Hall Trail, an icy shower and a shot of tequila later, and Laramie was ready. He dropped onto the couch in his cabin, thrust his legs out in front of him and grabbed the phone. He never used the landline, wasn't here to talk to people. Maybe the battery was dead.

He held it to his ear, grimaced at the dial tone, then dialed Sammi's number.

He wasn't avoiding temptation he assured himself as the phone rang. He wasn't at all concerned at what might happen if his news caused her to cry, tempting him to pull her into his arms for comfort. He was saving her the embarrassment of having to explain his presence if he went into town to give her his news in person.

Laramie hunched lower on the couch and shook his head.

God, he was doing a whole lot of lying to himself lately.

Before he could debate the merits and drawbacks of this new form of self-deception, Sammi answered.

"Hello."

"Sammi Jo."

"Laramie." The word was breathy with curiosity, hesitation and a hint of embarrassment. "Did you find out anything?"

He hesitated.

"Just confirmed a few things, filled in a few blanks. Nobody around here seems to have reason to kidnap Barclay or suspicions of anyone who would." He drummed his fingers on his knee and debated. Then, because he figured she deserved it, he went with the truth. Or, at least, some of it. "He doesn't have much in the way of admirers around here, or respect for that matter."

"Oh."

He heard a creaking he recognized as bedsprings and almost groaned. Trying not to picture her in bed, not to wonder what she was wearing, Laramie filled her in on the rest of the details. Well, almost the rest. He couldn't quite bring himself to tell her she was being cheated on. He'd planned to. He meant to. But, dammit, she sounded devastated enough hearing Barclay was an ass. Maybe it was better to let that sink in before hitting her with the rest.

With that in mind, Laramie straightened upright, ready to end the call.

"You don't like him, either, do you? Sterling, I mean. I can tell when you talk about him." There was no censure in her tone, no accusation in her words. Just simple curiosity.

Curious himself, Laramie settled back into his slouch.

"I haven't seen the man in over a dozen years. My views are based on old impressions and probably not accurate," he pointed out.

"Are you avoiding answering?"

Laramie grinned at the irritation in her words. He could imagine the look on her face, that chin raised up and her pretty green eyes narrowed.

"I never liked the guy's attitude," Laramie finally admitted. "He had everything right there at his fingertips. Instead of appreciating that, he'd take what little others had."

"Did he take something from you?" she asked.

Laramie frowned as he actually felt sympathy coming through her quiet words.

"Sammi Jo, do you actually think anyone ever took anything from me?"

Before the words had left his mouth, though, his gaze shifted to the window and the copse of trees beyond sheltering his mother's grave. She'd been taken from him, but he didn't figure life counted.

"But you haven't seen Sterling in years. Don't you think people can change?"

"No." His laugh was a little bitter as Laramie looked around the cabin where he'd spent most of his early years. How many promises had been made in this very room? Vows to quit drinking so much, promises to spend time with the family. To be more responsible, to quit blowing the rent money, to be in town for a father-son camping trip.

Not one of those promises or the hundreds of others had been kept.

"Never?" Her tone was filled with chiding doubt.

"Not without a drill sergeant riding their ass. And they still slide right back into their old habits the minute the threat of AWOL is lifted."

"I changed," she pointed out stiffly. "And I didn't have a drill sergeant or any threats hanging over my head."

"Sammi Jo, you might have grown up, but you're exactly the same as you were when you were a kid." Laramie grinned at her gasp. It didn't take a genius to catch the clue that he'd insulted her.

"You're still as feisty and strong as you were taking on bullies when you seven," he said, starting to relax as he enjoyed himself. "You still stand up for yourself and you believe in happy endings. Your hair is darker, but it's still vividly unique. You're gorgeous in a way that sets you apart from others. You're patient and you're kind. You follow the rules even when you don't want to and you're too responsible for your own good."

Realizing he was a sentence or two away from sounding like a lovestruck idiot, Laramie clamped his mouth shut. He had never said anything so revealing to a woman before. Outside of duty, he wasn't sure he'd ever actually said that much at one time in his life.

The words hung in the air, mocking him.

But, fist shut tight in his lap, Laramie couldn't wish them back. Not if they helped Sammi see how amazing she was just being herself.

"You make me sound a lot more interesting than I am," she said quietly. Then he heard the mattress creak again. Good. His body loosened a little. He'd do better if he wasn't imagining her in bed. He could hear the soft echo of her bare feet pacing what sounded like a wooden floor. "Except for the rule following. That sounds a little uptight."

She said it as if it was an insult.

"I wouldn't say it's—"

"I'm not uptight," she interrupted. "Rules and responsibility are important, but that doesn't mean I don't know how to have fun."

His rumbling stomach telling him it was time to eat, Laramie pushed to his feet. Normally he'd use dinner as an excuse to end the call, but he was enjoying talking with Sammi too much.

"I didn't imply—"

"Just because security and stability are important to me doesn't mean I'm a stick-in-the-mud prude. I can do plenty of fun, nonuptight things," she interrupted again.

Bread in one hand, lunchmeat in the other, Laramie could only laugh.

"I never said—"

"You made me come." Her words slid over him in a sensual caress. His body heading straight for hard-on city, Laramie set the food on the counter. He had the feeling he was going to want both of his hands and all of his focus for the rest of this conversation.

"Sammi—"

"You made me feel amazing."

"You deserve to feel amazing," he said automatically. "Why does it surprise you?"

At her silence, an odd suspicion hit him.

"Sammi Jo, you've had sex before, haven't you?"

Her hesitance only added to his suspicion.

"Yes. A few times. A while ago." She huffed. "It wasn't very good, if you must know."

"How long is *a while ago*? A week? A month?"

She mumbled something indistinct.

"Say that again?"

"Three years." The words weren't a whole lot louder this time, but they were distinct.

Food forgotten, Laramie dropped to the couch. His brain boggled at the idea of three months, let alone three years without sex. Sure, he supposed it was doable. But not for someone as sensually responsive as Sammi Jo.

"But you're engaged. Haven't you and Barclay…" He couldn't even say it. Not when the words might put the image in his mind of the lusciously sweet Sammi Jo with that cheating dumbass.

"No."

"Are you—" What was the term? "Saving yourself for your wedding night?"

"No. I mean, yes, we would then, but it's not like we're

saving it or anything." Her words were filled with frustration. Understandable, considering what she was saying. "We're just not that kind of couple."

"And you're willing to marry the guy?" All he could do was shake his head.

"I didn't think it mattered." Her voice dropped a couple of decibels. "I didn't think I was the sexual type."

Laramie had to figure that thinking was due to her growing up knowing more about sex than most guys he'd served with. A part of him wanted to end this conversation here and now, before his jeans got any tighter. But he couldn't let her go on thinking something that was so blatantly wrong.

"Sammi, I've been with a lot of women of damn near every sexual type," he said slowly, choosing his words as carefully as he'd choose tools to diffuse a bomb. "If I've learned nothing else, it's that everyone has their trigger. Something that opens the door to pleasure. If you haven't felt it yet, you simply haven't found the right key."

"Do you have it?" she asked, her words as soft as a butterfly kiss. "Are you holding the key?"

Brow arched, Laramie glanced down at the rock-hard erection straining his zipper.

"Because you're the first man who's made me feel these things. You're the first one who's made me want them."

God. She was killing him. Laramie shifted, angling his legs out straight in front of him to try to relieve the pressure against his zipper.

"Why do you think it's different with you?" she wondered. "Is it because of your reputation? Because you've done so many things and my body knows you're an expert?"

"You can feel the same pleasure without me," he said, only half lying but not willing to let her pin all of her sexual faith on him and him alone. "You just have to trust and let go."

"How?" She sounded as perplexed as if he'd suggested that she build a submarine to race across the Atlantic.

"Think about what turns you on."

"You do."

"Sammi." Undone by her honesty, he closed his eyes, his head dropping back on the couch. "Okay, then. Imagine how I turn you on. Just think about what I do that makes you feel good. Imagine me doing them to you."

He almost choked on his words when she gave a long, soft sigh. This was a mistake. He knew it was a mistake that he'd regret. But Laramie couldn't help it. He lowered his voice to a husky murmur and told her what he'd do, how he'd do it.

"Imagine my lips on your breasts. Think about what it'll feel like when I lick your nipples. When I nibble on one, then the other." He heard the bedsprings creak again and waited a beat. "Touch yourself, Sammi. Touch yourself the way you imagine me touching you. Just close your eyes and feel."

By the time he'd told her how he'd lick his way up her thigh, he heard her breath quicken, then shudder. It was all he could do not to reach into his pants and give himself the same pleasure. Except pleasuring himself while talking phone sex to Sammi was one step away from having real sex with her. And he was pretty sure the only resistance he had left was that single step.

Laramie's fist constricted, his body screaming for release.

He wanted to show her how good it'd feel. He wanted to take her in every way he knew how and let her see for herself just how good she was at it.

But he wasn't sure whom that would cause more trouble

for. Sammi, who'd have to live with that knowledge while married to an ass like Barclay. Or himself, who'd have to live without Sammi.

"Look, I'm going to take a couple days, go to San Antonio to look for Barclay," he decided on the spot before she could recover enough to speak. "He lived there for years. Whatever trouble he's in probably started there."

And he needed to put a little distance between himself and temptation.

Because if he made Sammi Jo come one more time, he wasn't going to be able to stop until he'd stripped them both naked and satisfied them both at the same damned time.

MMM, CHOCOLATE.

Rich, decadent and oh, so fulfilling.

Sammi Jo eyed the slice of triple-fudge delight with all of the pent-up desire in her system. The glass display case held other baked treats. Glistening éclairs, cream-topped mousse and tarts ripe with sugared fruit.

But Sammi only had eyes for the cake.

She'd bet it tasted amazing. That each bite would bring its own special kind of satisfaction. She felt as if she'd discovered a whole new world of needs, of desires. And now she was desperate to gratify each and every one.

She breathed deep the sweet air, thinking of the source of all of those desires.

Laramie.

He was still away, but he'd called every night for the past three nights.

And she'd come.

Every night for the past three nights.

Each night their call had been more intense, more sexually focused. Each night he'd pushed her to explore her sensuality with suggestions on what she should do to herself. How she should touch herself. Ways to intensify the pleasure he'd taught her to build.

She gave a little shudder as the memory of last night's phone call kindled a flame of desire low in her belly.

"Sammi Jo, are you paying attention?"

No, dammit.

Sammi drew in a deep breath, trying to control the urge to scream.

She was deliberately not paying attention. For all the good it was doing, she wanted to ignore everything that had anything to do with the wedding. Because thinking about it forced her to face the increasing surety that marrying Sterling was a mistake.

She wanted some time, some distance to figure this out. To know if her doubts were real or if they were simply a reaction to everything that was happening.

But as with everything else to do with this three-ring circus of an event, it wasn't about what Sammi wanted.

So, after one last little shudder of need, she reluctantly turned away from the glass display.

"You prefer the white cake with white buttercream and no filling," Sammi said, repeating the coordinator's choice in a monotone. She gave the baker a polite smile, not wanting the woman to think she had anything against her white cake with buttercream frosting. Except boredom, of course.

"It looks lovely." And bland. "But we're here for the tasting, aren't we? So shouldn't we consider the other options? Maybe actually taste them?"

"Of course." The sprite smiled a little wisp of a smile, then gestured with a surprisingly large hand toward a lovely table set for two. On the rose-hued tablecloth were two plates, and between them a tiered crystal stand, each of the levels holding at least four slices of cake.

"Gorgeous," Sammi declared, almost clapping her

hands in delight. What better distraction from her crazy thoughts than dessert?

Sammi started to slide into one of the delicate ice cream parlor chairs. Before her butt could land, though, Mrs. Ross clapped her hands as if smacking the very notion from Sammi's mind.

"You are not here to gorge yourself on cake, Sammi Jo. The flavors have been chosen. You are here to approve them."

Her eyes locked with the other woman's, Sammi inclined her head, then with great deliberation, sat. She crossed one leg over the other and leaned back in the chair. Mrs. Ross's warning was music to her ears.

"Would you care to join me?" she invited, gesturing to the empty chair.

"Oh, but this seat is for your fiancé." Mrs. Dias flicked a glance at the frowning woman hovering over the vanilla cake. "Would you like me to bring a third chair?"

"No, thank you, though. My fiancé won't be joining us." He wouldn't have joined them even if he'd been next door, she realized. Sterling had shown virtually no interest in the details of the wedding. Of course, she hadn't been much better. Maybe that was part of the problem, she realized. Maybe if she were more invested in the event, she'd have fewer doubts about going through with it.

"Mr. Barclay was quite specific about which cake is to be served."

Did the woman go to bed each night journaling the immortal instructions of Mr. Barclay?

Deciding discretion was the better part of valor and that a full mouth tended to shout less, Sammi accepted a fork from the baker. After careful consideration, she chose the lighter of the two samples of chocolate cake.

She didn't even get her fork into it before Mrs. Ross

whipped the plate out from under her and replaced it with the slice of vanilla.

"This is the cake that was approved. This is the cake you're here to taste."

For a brief, oh-so-satisfying second, Sammi imagined herself picking up that plate of dry white cake with its boring white frosting and smashing it in the other woman's face. But the baker was staring with an avid expression, her eyes bouncing from one to the other as if she were taking notes.

Sammi stiffened, hot color warming her cheeks as her brief rebellion was smothered by the dread of being gossiped about.

"I'm sure we can reach a compromise," she said stiffly.

"This is a traditional wedding and the cake will be a classic white as is customary." The woman leaned closer, her voice as quiet as the air so that only Sammi could hear as she continued, "I was hired to ensure that this wedding reflects the taste and breeding of the Barclay name. I will not allow anything to mar that image."

Was that because the woman was hell-bent on protecting her vision of the wedding, and in doing so, her reputation? Sammi's eyes narrowed. Or had Mr. Barclay indicated that he didn't think Sammi Jo had taste or breeding? Was this how she was going to spend her married life? With someone watching over every decision, every move because she wasn't capable?

But Sammi just nodded. After all, what else was she going to do?

"Of course I understand." Her smile was tiny and stiff. Then she turned to the sprite in the white apron. "Mrs. Dias, can you box up all of the samples please?"

After a brief glance at Mrs. Ross, the baker gave Sammi

a quick nod and flitted behind the display counter. While she gathered boxes, Sammi pulled out her wallet.

"What do you think you're doing?"

"Mrs. Dias went to a great deal of trouble to provide all of these lovely samples. Since you've deemed them all off-limits for my wedding, I'm taking them home with me." Absently noting that outrage wasn't pretty on the other woman, Sammi pulled out the inn's credit card. "After all, if the Barclay Inn is going to feature weddings, we should have a variety of options, shouldn't we?"

"But… But…" the woman sputtered, her face turning a scary shade of purple. "That's ridiculous. If I'm to co-ordinate, I will provide whatever options are necessary."

"Mmm-hmm." She nodded when Ms. Dias lifted up a white bakery bag to see if Sammi wanted the boxes in it. Then, her smile still in place thanks to her clenched teeth, Sammi looked back at Mrs. Ross. "Except your idea of necessary and the brides' might be quite different."

"My agreement is with Mr. Barclay. You have absolutely no say in it," the older woman pointed out in a tone so bitchy that even Mrs. Dias cringed.

How well she knew that fact. Sammi had read the contract forward, backward and three ways sideways. She might be stuck with the woman, but only within certain parameters.

"Your contract stipulates that for the first year of Weddings at Barclay, you are the exclusive coordinator for said events." Accepting the charge slip and pen the baker handed her, Sammi waited a beat before offering her sweetest smile. "But not everyone needs—or wants—a coordinator. Some people might have their own visions for their wedding. Some people might want their day to reflect their tastes. And as the one who will be explaining all of their options and choices to these happily-to-be-married couples, I'll have firsthand knowledge of which to suggest."

Sammi signed her name with a flourish before taking her bag of cake. A nod of thanks for the baker and she was done.

"Something to think about," she told the gaping steam-roller of a wedding coordinator just before she sailed out of the bakery, her bag of oral delight in hand.

8

ALL HE'D WANTED was his three weeks of peace and solitude. No people, no stress, no demands.

Instead, he'd walked way too many steps down memory lane to revisit a past he'd preferred to ignore, talked to more people in five days than he usually did in a month and spent three days driving halfway across Texas and back.

And become obsessed with a woman about to marry another man.

As he turned off the highway toward Jerrick, Laramie gave brief consideration to driving on through to El Paso and catching a flight home.

But Sammi Jo was waiting.

After their phone calls over the past three nights, he didn't plan on keeping either of them waiting any longer. Because, damn, those had been some great phone calls.

He was surprised that it wasn't the sexual elements of the calls that stood out in his mind. It was the conversations. The shared thoughts and laughter. Maybe it was because those had been the first phone conversations he'd ever had with a woman that lasted longer than three minutes, but he hadn't realized that he'd had so much to say.

Laramie shook his head as Alan Jackson gave way to

Luke Bryan on the radio. Finding out that he could talk for hours was nothing compared to the shock of discovering how interested he was in what Sammi had to say. And when she'd started talking sex again? Hot damn. Laramie turned up the air conditioner. Just thinking about it was getting him hard once more.

Knowing danger when he was getting off to the sound if its voice, he'd decided not to call Sammi the next night.

But when his cell phone had rung while Laramie was searching for sleep on the too-soft motel bed, he'd answered. Instead of Barclay, they'd talked about their jobs. About her dream of traveling someday, about his pride in being a SEAL. They'd discussed favorites and shared their taste in everything from food to music to holidays.

And then, of course, they'd had phone sex.

Laramie slowed as he hit Main Street, wondering what it was about Sammi that had him acting so out of character. Was it like an illness? Something short-term that he'd get over after some mutually naked bed rest? Or was it fatal?

Since thinking about it was giving him a headache, Laramie did the unthinkable. He ignored the problem. Instead, relying on gossip and a few vague memories for directions, he parked his truck in the lot behind Fiona's Arts & Crafts, skirting through the alley toward the back of the inn. He checked cars as he went to be sure they were empty, then after testing the garden gate to ensure its silence, set foot on Barclay property for the first time in years.

And, dammit, lightning didn't shoot from the sky.

Resigned to disappointment when it came to this town, Laramie paused inside the gate to listen, then, his senses on full alert, he moved silently through the night-darkened garden, taking care to stick to the shadows. As far as he was concerned, he'd already seen too many people. The last thing he wanted was to be seen by anyone. Especially not visiting Sammi's place late at night.

No point screwing her life up when he was pretty sure he'd recover from whatever this thing was that had a hold on him.

He made his way toward what had once been a garage. The same creamy white as the inn, the space that'd previously held two cars in a tight fit was now apparently Sammi's apartment. He knocked, but there was no response. Laramie scanned the perimeter one more time before checking the door. When the handle twisted open he stepped inside and looked around.

Damn. The last time he'd seen a place this small was when he'd spent the better part of two years living cramped like a sardine in a submarine. It sure smelled a lot better in here, though. Like a mix of spiced flowers, something sweet and that scent that was Sammi's own.

The base of the walls was a rich golden yellow that faded into the color of butter by the time it reached the ceiling. He'd stepped into the kitchen, if the stove and fridge were anything to go by. A bottle of wine stood breathing on the counter and a bowl of fruit sat on top of the fridge but there was no table. Instead, a long counter spanned the length of the room. At this end, there were a couple of bar stools tucked under it; halfway down it held a flat-screen television and at the other end a sensual twist of metal that, since it curved toward the bed, was a reading light.

His gaze lingered on the bed. The iron headboard featured two entwined nudes in a soft green patina that contrasted with the rich purple spread and enough pillows for a platoon scattered in inviting disarray.

Even as his body tightened, hard and wanting, he had to laugh. From the framed watercolor of a bleeding sunset to the plush, backless couch in vivid red to the sex-inviting bed, the place screamed sensuality.

And Sammi thought she'd be okay in a bland marriage to a dickless wonder like Barclay?

With perfect timing, the door at Laramie's back swung open and in came Sammi. Balancing a huge tray in her hands, she looked guiltily over her shoulder before nudging the door shut with her foot.

Laramie grinned, warm pleasure surging at the sight of her. With her hair piled on top of her head like an autumn rose and tumbling around her face, she looked ready for bed. Which was fine with him. In a threadbare white T washed so many times that he could see every detail of her bra, right down to the tiny yellow flowers along the cup, and frayed cutoffs it was obvious that Sammi hadn't been expecting company.

Good. His eyes lingered on her cleavage, the shadowy fullness making his mouth water. Less chance they'd be interrupted.

"I hope whatever you've got on that covered tray is enough to feed two." Laramie stepped away from the shadowed side of the fridge. "I'm starving."

Sammi's shriek shot through the small space. Laramie stepped forward in case he had to catch the tray—he really was starving—but Sammi's reflexes were solid. Instead of tossing it high, she gripped the handles in a way that told him if she hadn't recognized him, she'd be using it as a weapon against his head.

"Laramie." She dropped the tray onto the two-burner stove with a loud clatter, then pressed both hands to her chest as if trying to stop her heart from jumping right out. "You scared me. I didn't know you were back."

"I just got into town." And had had to see her. Wanted to touch her. Desperately needed her.

For the first time in his life, suddenly Laramie wasn't sure of himself. What did he say to her? How did he approach her? Sure, they'd shared a few orgasms. But those had been some unusual circumstances and the fact was that this was Sammi Jo, who was technically engaged to another man.

When she opened her mouth, then closed it again without saying anything, his discomfort increased. That's when Laramie noticed how swollen and red her eyes were.

Tension slammed through his body, putting his senses on full alert. Fists tight, he put himself between Sammi's body and the door.

"What happened?" He'd checked the perimeter and the premises when he arrived, but Laramie did another scan before inspecting Sammi from head to toe. That he didn't see any signs of violence didn't mean she hadn't been assaulted. "Are you okay?"

"You look like you're about to do serious hurt on someone." Looking fascinated now instead of dejected, Sammi gave him a wide-eyed stare. She reached as if to touch his cheek, but before making contact she tightened her hand into a fist and let it drop to her side. "Did you find Sterling?"

And just like that, all of the anticipation and that little spark of hope in Laramie shut down. Ignoring the tight feeling in his chest, he carefully stepped back, putting a few feet between them.

"I didn't find Barclay."

"Oh." Her deep breath pressed her breasts tight against the threadbare fabric of her smiley-face T, the move lifting the shirt away from the waistband of her denim cutoffs. Laramie's mouth went dry. "Did you have anything for me, then?"

Oh, the many responses that ran through his head.

He had to take a mental step back, chanting cadence in his head to keep his mind off them. Because unlike her actions while in an alcohol-induced haze, or over the safe distance of the phone, she'd made it clear that she wasn't interested in what he had to offer.

"I didn't find Barclay," he repeated with a shrug. "He's safe, though. And I know why he was grabbed and who's behind it."

So many emotions chased one another across that expressive face. Frustration, hope, fear and, surprisingly, anger. It was that last one that Laramie addressed.

"Why does that piss you off?"

For a second she looked as if she were going to protest, to claim that she wasn't angry, and Laramie mourned that fury-fueled eight-year-old who'd never hesitated to use her fists to solve things.

"Me? Pissed?" Sammi threw her hands in the air, the move pulling that shirt tight across her jiggling breasts and Laramie almost groaned. Nope. The eight-year-old had been kick-ass, but he'd take the twenty-four-year-old any day. "Why should I be pissed? I'm stuck here pretending everything is fine while my fiancé is missing. I've had three bridal showers, each one more embarrassing than the last."

She shot him a narrow-eyed look so filled with outrage that Laramie had to force himself not to laugh.

"Do you know what a Brazilian is?" She poked a finger in the air before he could respond that it was a person from Brazil. "It's something that hurts, that's what it is. It's embarrassing and painful. And there I was at my stupid spa shower, stuck stripping those fancy panties they foisted on me at the last party, so some masochist with a hair fetish could pour hot wax on me and then rip it right back off. All because I couldn't offer an acceptable excuse not to."

Oh.

Laramie's lips twitched.

That kind of Brazilian.

His gaze dropped to her shorts, wondering what shape was hidden beneath that worn denim. He'd seen hearts, lightning bolts, sports logos, diamonds and once enough bling to make him think twice about getting too close.

"Why didn't you just say no?" he managed to say instead of asking if she'd considered a question mark.

"How?" She shot him an impatient look. "As far as they all know, Sterling is hale and hearty in Dallas instead of kidnapped by God knows who for God knows what until God knows when. So I couldn't tell them that I'm having second thoughts about getting married. Who does that? Who ditches a guy while he's being held captive?"

One who would have ditched him, anyway, Laramie wanted to suggest. But he wasn't sure Sammi was ready to hear that. Instead, he pulled one of the stools out from under the room-length counter and settled in to get comfortable.

"Why couldn't you tell them you preferred to go with what nature provided? Or that Barclay prefers it." It was killing him not to stare at her shorts while saying that. Curiosity was so intense he had to actually force himself to resist the urge to talk her into letting him get a closer look at the subject of their discussion.

"Because these women believe that it's a bride's duty to make herself as sexually attractive as possible to her new husband." Sammi rolled her eyes with the same disgust echoed in her tone. "As if whoever she was when he proposed wasn't good enough or something."

"Do you really care what all those women think?"

That stopped Sammi Jo in her tracks.

"What difference does that make?"

Laramie scowled. Did she really believe that? His mother's oft-stated words came to mind.

"To thine own self be true." When Sammi's mouth dropped a little, he quickly added, "The difference between being happy and subverting your preferences to fit into someone else's standard."

Frowning, Sammi opened her mouth, then closed it again as if she didn't know how to respond. Finally, her brow still creased in a sharp line, she shrugged.

"Standards or not, the deed is done. I'm plucked, waxed and oiled."

All of the blood in his body shot straight to his dick at that image.

"Then, as if that weren't enough, I had to sit through lunch afterward feeling as if everyone in the restaurant knew what I looked like under my panties." She grimaced, her voice dropping painfully. "On top of it all, who should come in during dessert while everyone was sharing their favorite honeymoon sex stories but Janette Glass. It was as if someone had filled the room with hissing snakes, the way the room exploded in whispers. I wanted to crawl under the table."

Janette Glass. Laramie's amusement faded and understanding dawned. His stomach tightened, reminding him why he'd always been content to keep relationships with women purely sexual. He didn't know if this was the sort of thing that he was supposed to offer an emotional supportive hug or if he should do what he'd wanted to all week, and offer to kick Barclay's ass.

"How'd you find out?" was all he could manage.

"Find out that my fiancé has a lover? I've known for a while." Sammi shrugged, her expression making it clear that she wasn't going to talk about it.

Did she know about the others, too? He leaned back on

the stool, debating. This was his opening, free and clear, to make a real move on her. But he couldn't. Not when she was this vulnerable. Instead, he'd fill her in on what he'd learned about Barclay, then he'd get the hell out of here.

Laramie rubbed the back of his thumb over his forehead, wondering if he should see the base shrink when he got back to Coronado. Because something was seriously wrong with him.

"Look, you have every right to be upset that the man you're planning to marry is sleeping with someone else," he finally pointed out.

"What?" Looking confused for a second, Sammi then shook her head. "Oh, that? Well, I'd rather he wasn't, but according to Sterling, we're not married yet."

Whoa. What the hell difference did that makc? A commitment was a commitment. Before he could say that, though, Sammi shrugged.

"Besides, aren't I practically having one of my own?"

"Whoa, sugar." Sliding to his feet, he lifted one hand in protest. "Don't be owning what isn't yours. A couple of kisses and some naughty talk aren't an affair."

She stopped midpace to shoot him a chiding look.

"I practically threw myself at you both times we kissed," she reminded him with that refreshing honesty he admired so much. Even as hot color washed her cheeks and her words lowered to a whisper, she continued. "And I came. That time in the alley, and each time we talked on the phone. Each time. What do you call that?"

"A credit to how good I am." He tipped his hat back with his knuckles.

WELL, SHE COULDN'T deny that.

Sammi gave a helpless laugh.

Just looking at him standing there with his hat tilted

back and that cocky grin on his face was enough to get her excited. The hard planes of his cheeks were dusted with a couple days' growth, giving him an extrasexy air of danger.

How was she supposed to ignore that allure?

She'd come in his arms while he was fully dressed and he hadn't been interested enough in more to even remove his hat.

She'd had phone sex with the man three nights in a row, each one hotter than the last for her. But for him? If his reaction to seeing her again was anything to go by, he'd probably been watching TV during those calls.

She'd even told the man about her bikini wax—although she hadn't actually intended to blurt that out. Had that got his attention? Obviously not.

Very conscious of her ratty hair and bedraggled appearance, Sammi looked around, desperate for a distraction.

Aha.

She grabbed two glasses from the cabinet above the sink, adding them and the bottle of wine to her tray. Before she could lift it, Laramie was there, taking it for her.

"Where to?"

Sammi debated telling him she wanted it in bed, then with a sigh gestured toward the couch. He'd made it clear that he wasn't interested, and she really didn't think she could handle another rejection.

"Are you still here next week?"

"Part of it." Laramie paused in the act of setting the tray on the low glass table to give her a questioning look. "Why?"

Sammi tried to gauge the resilience of her ego as she curled up on the corner of the low-slung red leather couch. She was still smarting too much to tell, though. Maybe once she'd dealt with the fallout from one rejection, she'd know if she could handle another.

With that in mind, she leaned forward to pour wine into one glass, and after getting a nod from Laramie, the other. She waited until he'd parked his hat on the table and settled on the opposite end of the couch, far enough away that she had to stand again to give him his drink.

"So what's the deal with Sterling?" she asked once she'd settled back on the couch, tucking her feet under her. "You said you knew what was going on."

"That partner of his, Dillard is up to his ass in debt. He took out a loan from the kind of people who collect late fees with weapons. He's been siphoning funds from the car dealership, but when Barclay got suspicious he corrupted the computer system to try to buy time."

"That's why Sterling was using my computer," Sammi exclaimed as realization dawned. "To try to check the dealership's books."

"Probably. He also froze the accounts."

"So Sterling is innocent? He didn't do anything wrong, but Carl Dillard kidnapped him?"

"Nothing I found on Barclay showed him dirty. But I'm not a PI, so there's probably a lot that I missed." Laramie shrugged off the idea of Sterling's innocence as if he'd never believe it. "Dillard has liquidated everything he's got and is in the wind. My take is the loan shark has Barclay. The only piece that doesn't make sense is his covering Dillard's ass by keeping the kidnapping a secret."

"He must not want his father to know." Sammi rubbed her forehead, wondering how she was going to smooth this one over between father and son. "Mr. Barclay dislikes—strongly dislikes—Carl. But the more he criticized the partnership, the more Sterling was determined to make it work."

"So let's see if I've got this right." Laramie leaned back, resting his booted foot on his knee and spreading his arms wide along the back of the low leather couch. His laid-back appearance was at odds with the cutting edge of his tone. "He pulled you into his kidnapping, worried you so much that you were willing to do anything, even barter your innocence, because he didn't want his old man knowing he was right?"

"Well—"

"He's such an arrogant jackass that he couldn't deal with the situation like a man. Instead he hides behind your skirt, putting you through hell and worry," Laramie stated. He went on and on, pointing out Sterling's each and every flaw in that same biting tone.

Since Sammi couldn't actually disagree with anything he said, she just let it roll right over her as she drank her wine and secretly reveled in the fact that someone was outraged on her behalf. Finally, after he'd been silent for a solid ten seconds, simply staring at her with an impatient look on that sexy face, she shrugged.

"I wasn't bartering my innocence," Sammi muttered into her glass as she finished her wine. After all, it was really the only thing she could disagree with.

For a moment he looked as if he were going to contest it. Or at least debate the definition of innocence. Then, apparently done with it, Laramie nodded.

"What were you going to do?" He gave her refilled glass an arch look. "Drown your worries in wine?"

"I was more embarrassed than worried," Sammi reminded him, wrinkling her nose before gesturing to the tray still covered with a silver dome. "The wine was just to wash this down with."

She lifted the lid, letting the comforting scents wrap around her like a warm hug. Covering three large plates were at least twenty slices of cake. Varying in size, color and texture, the glistening white frosting of one nestled up against the sassy pink-coated chocolate of another.

She waited expectantly.

After giving the tray a blank stare, he lifted that same stare to Sammi's face. She had to bite back her giggle when he wordlessly arched his brow.

"I had to visit the baker today to finalize the wedding cake order and had a craving for a taste," she explained with a loving look at her choices. After careful perusal, she chose a small plate with three squares of chocolate cake. Milk, mocha and double fudge, if she remembered correctly. "I've heard this thing about oral gratification. I'm trying it out."

As the rich scent of chocolate filled the air, she scooped up a bite too big for the fork, one hand under it to catch any crumbs. Sammi paused with the fork halfway to her mouth when Laramie closed his eyes and groaned.

"What? A lot of my friends use the phrase all the time. They say eating something takes their mind off their worries. Like just popping it into their mouth makes their whole world better."

More than ready to test the theory, Sammi nipped the cake off the fork. Mmm, yes. Chocolaty richness filled her mouth. So good. She wrapped her lips around the fork, sucking off the ganache that'd stuck to the tines.

"The creamy part is best," she commented, her eyes on the other cake options on her plate. Milk or mocha? Which had the most frosting? She was going to need a lot of frosting to get her through the fact that the man she wanted most in her life was sitting so far away from her that he probably had one cheek hanging off the edge of the red leather.

"Are you trying to kill me?"

Sammi wished she could ask him the same question.

"Did you want some? I can share?"

"Is this really how you're going to deal with it?" He shook his head. "Eat your way into a sugar coma?"

"Maybe I'm not eating cake because I'm upset about Sterling." Laramie sighed when she licked the frosting off her thumb. "Maybe I'm eating cake because I'm trying not to think about something else. Or maybe I'm eating it because I'm tired of people telling me what I can and can't do and what parts of my body should be waxed while doing or not doing it."

Sammi stabbed her fork into the air to emphasize each word before scooping up the milk-chocolate-covered slice.

"Sammi Jo." He reached over to lay one hand on her arm, keeping her from stuffing more cake in her mouth. The feel of his hand on her bare skin sent shivers of need through her. "Don't make yourself sick over Barclay. He's not worth it."

Sammi didn't know what came over her.

Maybe it was because Laramie had moved closer. Close enough to touch.

Or maybe it was chocolate going to her head, triggering an addictive need for more kinds of pleasure.

Or maybe it was simple frustration brought on by having the man of her fantasies touchably close but not interested in having her touch him.

But suddenly all of the frustrations, all of the sexual needs, all of the wishes unmet in her head exploded into a single act of defiance as Sammi dipped her fingers into her plateful of thick chocolate frosting and swiped then across Laramie's cheek.

Uh-oh.

Sammi's heart raced. Eyes wide, she fought with all her might to keep her expression neutral.

Slowly, his eyes never leaving hers, Laramie lifted his hand to wipe at the gooey smear on his cheek. He finally glanced at the chocolate on his fingers, contemplated, then looked at her again.

His expression still hadn't changed.

Sammi wasn't having as much luck with hers. She tried to look contrite, but the giggles kept bubbling up in her throat.

"Sorry," she finally managed, the word accompanied by an embarrassing snort of laughter. "I couldn't resist."

"Is that a fact? Well then, you leave me with no choice," he said in a considering tone.

"Sure I do," she protested, scooting backward on the couch. "There are plenty of choices available. Why don't we talk about them?"

"Haven't you heard? I'm not much of a talking kind of guy."

Moving so fast that she barely had time to blink, Laramie grabbed her. One arm wrapped around her waist to keep her from escaping, he showed her his frosting-smeared finger. There wasn't enough there to do damage, Sammi noted, relaxing a little.

In that uncanny way he had of reading her thoughts, Laramie reached over and swiped all of the lush, fluffy frosting off the chocolate cream cake.

"Hey, I was saving that," Sammi protested. "It's my favorite."

"Yeah?"

He wiped his chocolate-covered fingers across her face, from cheek to chin, before she could duck. Then, wicked amusement in his eyes, he dabbed what was left on her mouth.

In her own swift move, Sammi grabbed his hand, holding it in place so she could lick the frosting from his fingers. Flavors exploded, rich and decadent. Silken chocolate with just a hint of spice.

And Laramie.

"You need to be careful, Sammi Jo," he murmured, his eyes locked on hers. But he didn't pull away. "Otherwise you might find you're biting off more than you can chew."

Oh, the images that ran through her mind of all the things she could bite, nibble and lick.

"I'm so tired of being good," she whispered, holding his hand to her mouth before he could pull it away. Watching carefully, she ran her tongue along the side of his finger, her tongue swirling around and around before she sucked. Hard.

For a second, it looked as if Laramie was going to explode. His face tightened, his eyes heated. His breath came in a fast gasp.

Then, so fast she wondered if she'd imagined the passion, he closed it down. He gently pulled his hand from hers, released her waist and reached over to grab two napkins.

Sammi wasn't sure which was stronger. Disappointment or humiliation.

"You didn't like that?" she asked quietly, scrubbing the napkin over her cheek with more force than was necessary.

"I liked it too much," he corrected. "But you've taken a few hits, Sammi. I won't take advantage of your vulnerability and if you kept that up, I wouldn't have been able to stop myself."

"But what if it's not taking advantage?" She wet her lips, her tongue sipping away the last of the chocolate. "What if I want you to?"

For once, she could see what he was thinking. The concern over what he saw as her innocence. The reality that whatever happened here between then was all that would happen—there was no future for them. And desire.

Thankfully, he listened to the desire.

Laramie leaned in, taking her mouth in a kiss so hot, it turned her insides to lava. Sammi met his tongue, thrust for thrust. Her body delighted in the power of his kiss.

But even as wet heat pooled between her legs and her nipples beaded with need, his comment echoed in her mind. So, because it was Laramie and she could do anything with him, say anything to him, she pulled away to ask.

"Why are you doing this?"

Confusion clear on his face, Laramie shook his head.

"You want a list of reasons?"

"No. I don't need to see the list." She wet her lips. "I just want to know if pity is on it."

He gave a rough laugh.

"Sugar, you think I've been sporting a five-day hard-on for pity?" His eyes were hot as he wrapped his hand around hers and slid them down his body.

Oh, my.

Her fingers wide, Sammi ran her hand down the hard length behind his zipper. He was so big. Big and hard. She shivered.

She had to have him. She just had to.

"Then do things to me," Sammi murmured, letting her head fall back onto the couch so she could see his face. "Do the kind of things to me that I hear you do so well."

9

SAMMI JO WASN'T sure how it happened but in the space of time between her request and her next breath, she was laid out flat with her back on the floor.

And Laramie's body angled over hers.

Her bare legs tangled with the denim-clad length of his. Her hands gripped his shoulders, reveling in the hard, muscled flesh beneath his T-shirt.

Eyes wide, she stared up at him in wonder. Was this it? They were actually going to have sex? Should she take her shorts off? Or wait for him? Nerves danced through her body, overwhelming the passion with their nagging doubts.

Unsure of the moves but desperate to feel him touch her in the ways he'd talked about in their phone calls, Sammi's hand reached down to grab the hem of her shirt. Before she could pull it up, Laramie's hands were there, stopping her.

"I want to do that."

"Oh." Her uncertainty didn't have a chance against the needy excitement building inside, so Sammi gave a tiny shrug. Gesturing to the fabric he now held, she arched her brows. "Then go for it."

His face split in a delighted grin.

"Damned if I know why I keep expecting you to play the shy maiden. But it's a continual treat to realize I'm wrong."

"Is that what you prefer?" she wondered with a frown. With his reputation, she'd have thought he was more used to women who knew the sexual score than shy ones. Was she doing something wrong?

"I prefer you to be whatever you want to be." He skimmed one hand under her shirt, his palm warming her belly with yearning.

"I *prefer* that you act however you want to act." His hand skimmed higher. Sammi held her breath as his fingers traced the band of her bra just under the cup. She surreptitiously shifted higher, wanting more, needing more.

"I prefer that you be your genuine self, not who you think I expect you to be, or who anyone else has told you to be."

She managed to hold back her whimper of disappointment when he slipped his hand back out of her shirt but couldn't stop her bottom lip from dropping. Before she could protest, though, his fingers snagged the hem of her shirt and lifted.

Sammi's pout melted into a smile as he slowly pulled the fabric higher, exposing her belly. His knees still tight on either side of her hips, he leaned forward to press a whisper of a kiss to her bare flesh. She trembled at the sensation of his warm breath gliding over her. Unable to swallow past the knot in her throat, she watched him slide her shirt higher, the bright smiley face giving way to the shiny satin of her bra.

His eyes narrowed, a hint of a smile playing at the corner of his mouth. Sammi wordlessly arched her back, then raised her arms so he could pull the shirt free. Her eyes filled with wonder when, instead of tossing it aside, he bundled it carefully under her head as a pillow.

Focus on the physical, she warned herself. *It's nothing more than physical*. And thankfully, there was enough physical to occupy her complete attention.

Shivering at the contrast between her almost bare upper body when she was deliciously hot down below, Sammi reached out to pull Laramie to her.

But he shook his head.

"Not yet. Not until I'm ready. And I won't be ready until I drive you crazy, turn you inside out, then satisfy you. All while I watch," he said, his voice low and husky. "Then we're going to do the same thing all over again. To each other."

Sammi squirmed at the edgy need coiling low in her belly at his words. But what if she was already crazy? She was pretty sure if crazy was measured by unfulfilled needs, she was there.

"Then hurry," she demanded, cupping her own hands over her bra and squeezing in hopes of relieving some of the building pressure. "Because I can't wait much longer."

His grin flashed, fast and wicked.

He nudged the straps off her shoulders, pulling them down with fingers that traced a pattern on her arms until the straps were low enough to tug at the cups beneath her hands. Sammi made to release them, but Laramie pressed his own hands over hers.

Holding. Squeezing.

Tempting Sammi to tremble with need.

Still trapping her hands between his and her aching breasts, he slid a little lower, leaning down to nuzzle the sensitive curve of her throat. Her eyes drifting closed as the sweet delight swirled through her, Sammi angled her head to the side to give him better access.

His mouth was a wicked sort of magic, making her forget everything but how he made her feel as he scraped his teeth over the sensitive flesh of her throat, nibbling at her ear, then whispering kisses across her jawline until he reached her mouth.

Sammi's lips welcomed his. Their tongues tangled in an intimate dance, swirling and thrusting until she was ready to explode. Then he sucked her tongue into his mouth at the same time his fingers slipped under hers to skim under her bra, scraping her nipples.

Oh. Her breath caught in her throat. Her hands fell helplessly to her sides as she caught her bottom lip between her teeth and tried not to whimper.

Their mouths continued to slide together, hot and wet, in an erotic dance. Sammi wasn't aware that he'd removed her bra until he rubbed her nipples gently between his fingers.

Suddenly his fingers were gone. Before she could protest, she felt a cool stickiness coat her breast.

Her eyes popped open to see Laramie's half smile, his eyes intent. She glanced down to see that he'd chosen pink frosting to spread over her nipple, coating it with pastel sweetness. He swirled and dabbed the frosting with the intensity of an artist creating his masterpiece.

Sammi's body was so hot, she was surprised the frosting didn't melt all over her. Need curled, tight and wet, between her thighs. Her breath caught in her throat at the look on his face, at the feel of his fingers on her breast. Most of all, in anticipation of what he'd do once he was satisfied that he'd decorated her properly.

Finally, he leaned back, giving her breast a satisfied nod. Sammi bit her lip, waiting. The sticky concoction was drying, tightening just a little.

But still he didn't move.

"Laramie?" It came out a hoarse whisper, but Sammi had no pride at this point. Need had eaten it away.

"I think I want chocolate, too."

He repeated the process, spreading chocolate frosting over her other nipple. With every touch of his finger, the pebbled flesh quivered. Tiny bolts of pleasure shot through her until Sammi was actually squirming between his thighs.

Then he stopped.

Her eyes locked on his face; Sammi held her breath.

He leaned down. She sucked in her belly, lifting her chest closer. His breath warmed her skin, making her tremble.

Then he stopped again.

Sammi bit back a scream.

"Hang on." He straightened, both hands going to the bottom of his black shirt. Slowly, as if he knew it was killing her to wait, he lifted it up his belly, across his chest and over his head. "Didn't want to get frosting on my shirt."

The words were merely background buzz to Sammi.

Every atom of her being was focused on Laramie's chest.

Oh, oh, baby.

She let out a shaky breath.

She was pretty sure she'd just died and gone to heaven.

Because his body was too incredible to be that of a mere mortal.

Like a dull gold satin, his skin stretched over razor-sharp muscles honed to perfection. His shoulders ranged wide over a chest that was so cut she was surprised she hadn't seen the definition through his clothes. His arms—oh, his arms—were rounded concrete. And his abs. The light dusting of hair scattered across his chest, defining his flat nipples before running in a narrow line down the center of his belly where it disappeared into his jeans.

Sammi wanted to follow that trail until she really did find heaven. But first she had to pay homage to his abs.

She wanted to touch.

She needed to taste.

But when she shifted to do both, Laramie's hands pressed her back into the floor.

"I'm hungry," he murmured before following her down. "I just have to decide if I want to start with strawberry or chocolate frosting."

"Iced cherry," Sammi corrected breathlessly, giggling at his expression as he frowned from her face to her breasts and back again. "I'm usually all about the chocolate but the iced cherry is so amazing I couldn't decide which I liked better."

"Why don't you let me help you decide?" he suggested with a wicked smile.

Sammie's laughter faded. She'd been so in awe of his body that she'd forgotten about the frosting play. Now that she remembered, all she could feel was her nipples, their tight need and the erotically weird sensation of being frosted.

His legs slid along hers as he shifted lower, the scrape of denim against her sensitive bare flesh as exciting as his weight pressing down on her lower body.

Sammi lifted her hips, pressing tight against his chest in hopes of relieving some of the pressure building between her thighs. Always the gentleman, Laramie scooped one hand beneath her butt to help press her tighter, his fingers squeezing as he did.

Then he laved his tongue over her frosted nipple.

Sensations slammed through Sammi's body so hard, so fast, that she almost exploded. Her breath caught, trapped in her throat by a low moan of pleasure.

"Iced cherry is good," he murmured, the words an erotic rumble that she felt all the way to her core.

He had her other leg pinned, but Sammi was able to

raise one knee, pressing her foot into the floor as she tried to get closer.

He nibbled at the pebbled tip of her breast, each swirl of his tongue around the nipple sending her higher.

When he drew the wet, swollen bud into his mouth, sucking away the last of the frosting, Sammi moaned. Her hands raced over his bare flesh, reveling in the rock-hard satin of his muscles, gripping tight to biceps so big she couldn't wrap her fingers even halfway around them.

He switched to the chocolate-covered nipple, repeating the process of tongue swirling, teeth scraping, nibbling and licking delight. At the same time, he teased the wet, aching tip of the other until Sammi was light-headed with need.

She squirmed, trying to grip his leg between hers. As if realizing how close she was, Laramie shifted, sliding his thigh between hers, wedging it tight against the crux of her legs.

Sammi exploded.

Her body shook as stars exploded against the velvety black of her eyelids. Sensation after sensation whirled her around in dizzying circles of delight, taking her higher and higher with each tiny orgasmic aftershock.

While she was still quaking, Laramie's mouth covered hers. His tongue speared, deep and hard.

Even as Sammi went over again, she reveled in the rich cherry-chocolate flavor of the kiss. She felt as if she were floating on wave after wave of pleasure, slowly descending back into her body where all the good times were happening.

As she did, awareness slowly kicked in.

The hard floor against her back.

The air-conditioned draft cooling her skin.

Laramie's hot, hard body sliding along hers as he shifted

to his side. His fingers, trailing teasing hints of magic down her belly, skimming along her waistband.

Reaching for the button of her shorts.

Sammi's eyes flew open.

It took a strength she didn't realize she had to reach down and stop him.

Laramie's fingers stilled.

She felt, rather than saw his eyes study her face, forcing Sammi to slowly force hers open.

She had to work a little harder to find the words that were buried in her pleasure-fogged brain.

"Once you take my shorts off, I'll forget everything I want to do," she finally said, her words ending on a hot gasp when his finger dipped into her belly button. "I want to touch you first. I want to see you. To see how you look when you want me."

She bit her lip, waiting for his reaction. Would he object? Was he so far gone that he just had to get in there right this second? In her experience, he'd already outdone most guys' foreplay limits as it was.

But Laramie wasn't most guys.

As his slow, wicked grin confirmed.

He angled into a sitting position, making quick work of his boots and socks. Sammy pressed her hand to his bare back before he could lift his hips to do the same quick strip of his jeans. Reading her mind, he lay back on the floor, his head pillowed on one hand as he gave her the c'mere gesture.

Sammi shivered, feeling like a kid in a very well-built candy store. She turned onto her side and reveled in the freedom to taste every treat he had to offer.

Despite having come only moments before, her body was still tight with need. But this need was to act, not just to receive. To touch and taste and feel whatever she wanted.

She ran her palm over Laramie's cheek, murmuring with pleasure at the rough scrape of his end-of-day whiskers. His lips were so soft in comparison, his smile showing just a hint of indulgence. As if he knew this was the first time she'd had more than a cursory interest in a man's body and realized his was worthy of her attention.

She skimmed her hand down his chest, her fingers swirling, then flicking his nipple. She glanced up when it hardened.

"Does that feel as good for you as it does when you do it to me?" she wondered.

"It does feel good." His voice lowered to a sexy growl. "A few other things feel better."

Brow arched, Sammi smiled. She indulged in one more teasing flick, hoping they could do this again later so she could taste frosting off him. She flattened her palm against his chest, the soft hair rippling as she slid her hand lower. His body was simply gorgeous. Not an ounce of fat between those rock-hard muscles and the gold satin skin.

She shifted so one hand was propped flat on the floor, pressing herself up onto her hip so she could watch as she traced her finger over each ridge of his abdominal muscles. Excitement coiled tighter in her own belly the lower her fingers went.

Laramie simply lay there, letting her have her way. But a glance at his face proved he wasn't immune. His eyes were hot, his gaze intent on her hand. She could see his heart pounding harder in his throat. But the best proof of all was the rigid tightness pressing against his jeans.

Her pulse raced, her breath coming faster.

She shifted closer, her hair falling over her face as her breast brushed his side. Laramie sucked in a breath.

Sammi smiled, wide and satisfied.

For the first time in her life, she understood what feminine power was.

And she wanted more.

"Can I?" she asked softly, her fingers hovering over the button to his jeans.

"Sugar, you can do anything you want." Seeing the doubt in her eyes, he nodded. "Anything at all."

Her eyes round with delight, the excitement took on a whole new level of heat. Tense with anticipation, her gaze slid along the rigid length of his zipper, ideas racing through her mind. Before she could settle on which one she wanted to do first, he lifted one finger.

"On one condition."

Figures.

Sammi almost hissed, the disappointment was so intense. Leaning back on her elbow, she shoved her hair out of her face and waited.

"You can do anything you want," he repeated, his words low and deep as he slipped his hand behind her head and pulled her back down to him. "As long as you promise to tell me anything—everything—you want me to do to you."

Giddy with delight, she pressed a kiss to the hard flatness of his abs. She'd meant to move on to unzipping his jeans, but she couldn't resist a few more kisses. And licks. Her tongue followed the trail of hair, swirling and sipping her way down to his waistband. She flipped the snap and pulled the zipper down with one hand, the other smoothing that silken flesh.

She wanted to purr.

But she resisted.

But when she pulled back the denim, freeing the rigid length of his erection, she couldn't hold back her hum of appreciation.

Wow.

He was huge.

For a long moment she could only stare.

Sleek flesh speared high, the hardness thicker than her fist. The silken head beckoned, making her mouth water.

The idea of drooling on him pulled Sammi out of her trance. But didn't ease the need to taste.

Led by both passion and curiosity, she shifted closer. Before she tasted, she blew a puff of air over the silken head, smiling a little when Laramie's fingers slid into her hair.

He wanted her.

She ran her tongue around the head, sipping at the dewy proof. She ran the flat of her tongue down the shaft. Then up again before taking him into her mouth.

She wanted to suck. As need tightened in painful demand, she wanted to swallow him whole.

But Laramie had other ideas.

One sucking swish of her tongue and he angled himself into a sitting position, pulled her into his arms and took her mouth in a kiss so hot, so voracious that she'd swear he *did* swallow her whole.

His tongue thrust, his mouth demanding as his hands made faster work of her shorts than Sammi could have done herself. Her breath came in hard pants against his mouth as his fingers brushed over the sensitive flesh of her lower belly. She lifted her hips, helping him free her from the fabric.

It wasn't until she slid her legs against his, trying to wrap herself around him, that she realized he'd stripped his jeans away, too.

They were naked.

Together.

Why that made Sammi nervous all of a sudden was a mystery.

Just as she was about to suggest they move to the bed—where there were blankets—Laramie dipped his hand between her legs. The second his fingers touched her quivering nether lips, Sammi's nerves, her embarrassment and most of her thoughts simply disappeared on a wave of heady pleasure.

His fingers skimmed, swirled, teased while he took the kiss deeper. Sammi pressed closer, her hips undulating in time with his hand, needing more. Wanting everything.

Then he dipped inside her.

One finger. Two.

In.

And out.

That's all it took before Sammy exploded.

It was as if he'd lit a fuse, because her body simply ignited. She felt as if she were on fire, the heat of her orgasm was so intense. Her breath burned her throat; her heart pounded in her ears.

And she wanted more.

She wanted everything.

"In me," she panted. "In me. In me. Please, I need you in me."

Ever the gentleman, Laramie shifted.

Eyes closed, her back still arched to press her sensitive folds tighter against his fingers, she felt him move between her thighs. Sammi widened her legs, planting her feet and digging her heels into the floor. The need in her was so powerful, so intense that it bordered on pain.

Then she felt him pressing against her still vibrating lips.

Waiting.

Remembering how big he was, Sammi's eyes shot open.

As she stared up at Laramie, nerves trickled through her desire. His face was tight, his eyes fogged with passion.

Then he smiled. A sweetly reassuring smile so similar to the one he'd given her when they were kids that Sammi actually felt herself fall over the edge into love.

As she fell, Laramie leaned down to brush a gentle kiss over her lips. Then, his eyes locked on hers, he slowly slid inside.

Oh, God. Oh, God. Oh, God.

He was so deep.

So hard.

So perfect.

Sammi's breath shuddered, her hands sliding over his chest, along his shoulders, down his arms.

He slowly slid out, almost all the way. She tightened her legs, unwilling to let him go.

That was apparently the signal Laramie was looking for, because he slid in again, faster this time.

She gasped at the delicious friction.

He reached between them to cup her breast in one hand, his body balanced on the other as he continued his hard, deep slide in and out.

Each thrust pushed her higher, closer and closer to that elusive promise of pleasure. Nothing she'd ever felt before could compare. The orgasms he'd already given her were just teases, she realized. Leading up to something bigger. Something mind-blowing.

Something she had to have.

Now.

Her breath coming in sobbing gasps, Sammi grabbed hold of his hips, needing him to give her that final push.

"Please," she begged, arching her back so high that only her shoulders and head were still on the floor.

"Please, what?" Laramie teased, his words just a little

hoarse as he continued the delicious torture of those slow thrusts.

"Please, Christian," she groaned through teeth clenched tight.

Whether it was the need in her voice or that she'd used his given name, something flipped a switch.

And Laramie went wild.

His growl was low and intense, his face sharp as he pounded deeper. His fingers gripped her butt, holding her high for his sharp thrusts.

Sammi exploded, pleasure bursting into a thousand tiny pieces of ecstasy. Her vision went black as she gave a long, keening moan. Just as she felt she'd reached the peak, Laramie's fingers tightened.

His thrusts grew sharper. Jerkier.

He groaned, long and hard as his pleasure burst through her. She could hear his breath, hot and jagged, ripping through the air. As she tried to catch her breath, tried to find the will to open her eyes, he collapsed over her, their sweat-slicked bodies sliding together as he switched positions.

Sammi automatically curled against him, her head tucked into the curve of his throat.

Wow, was all she could think.

Just… *Oh, my God. Wow.*

DAMN IT ALL to hell.

His mind spinning counterpoint to his heart pounding a tribal rhythm in his head, Laramie tried to regulate his breathing.

But even as he tightened his hold on Sammi Jo, he couldn't think.

All he could do was feel.

And he felt incredible.

As he slowly drifted back to awareness, he tried to figure out why he felt so different.

She'd called him Christian.

Was that it?

She was the first woman he'd been with in probably a decade who even knew his given name. He'd like to think it was that added intimacy that had pushed it from great sex into mind-blowingly intense lovemaking.

Laramie had been with his share of women. Hell, according to a lot of the guys he knew, he'd been with their share, too.

But lying here with Sammi, the aftershocks of his orgasm still echoing through his system, he felt as if this had been his first time.

Crazy, was all he could think as she snuggled closer.

Eyes closed, acting on instinct, Laramie brushed his hand through the heavy, silken tangles of her hair.

Yeah. Thinking this sex had been better than any other he'd ever had, that was crazy thinking. He just might have to adjust to being crazy, he realized as he drifted off.

It might have been a half hour. It might have been a lifetime when he felt Sammi stir in his arms.

"Laramie?" Sammi asked, her mouth an erotic caress as she murmured the words against his chest. He was grateful that she was back to using his surname, and surprised she'd known he'd prefer it. Then he realized he shouldn't be. Sammi seemed to understand everything about him, to know everything there was to know.

"Yeah?" he finally drawled, opening his eyes to give her a look sleepy with passion.

"Are you done for the night?"

"Done?" His smile widened as he tangled his fingers in her silken hair. "Sugar, I don't think I'll ever be done with you."

Laramie automatically stiffened as the words left his mouth, his brain shouting a warning. Never say that sort of thing to a woman, it chided. That was the kind of thing that could be taken as a promise. For a man who never promised anything, those words were forbidden.

And never before in his life had he needed a reminder of that.

But Sammi was different.

He'd give Sammi anything. Including promises.

Before he could freak out at the realization, Sammi shimmied down his body, leaving a trail of hot temptation in her wake. Her hair tickled his thighs as she settled between them, her eyes wicked as she smiled up at him.

"I was just wondering if you liked this." She slowly traced her finger around the head of his erection. Around and around and around, swirling over the sensitive flesh. "Because I like this. Very much."

Her bold words were said with a smile, but Laramie could hear the shyness behind them.

"There isn't anything that you could do that I won't like," he said honestly, sliding his fingers into the silken fall of her fiery hair.

"It's never been like this," she confessed quietly, her gaze on her hand instead of meeting his.

Those words weren't anything new. Laramie had heard them plenty of times before. He'd always chalked them up to sex talk. A flattering sort of *thanks for the good time*.

But as with everything else, Sammi was different. Before he could tell her, though, she continued.

"I didn't get why everyone thought sex was such a big deal. It's not that I was a prude or anything." She looked up with a frown. "I mean, who could be raised the way I was and be a prude?"

"Maybe that's why you didn't think it was a big deal,"

he mused. "Because you were raised to see it as a commodity. Something cheap and easy to walk away from."

Even as he said that, Laramie realized that that's exactly how he'd always thought of sex. Something that felt good, something he had a healthy talent for. But it was something he walked away from without a single regret or a backward glance.

Except with Sammi.

Laramie's gaze roamed her face as he realized—and accepted—the fact that walking away from her would be filled with regrets.

"No, it's you that makes the sex special." She wet her lips before giving him a sincere smile. "You make it amazing. It's as if you're completely focused on each touch, on every move. You're like my dream lover."

Laramie's sexual skills, his talent in and out of bed, and his legendary gift with women had garnered a lot of praise over the years. But nothing had ever meant as much as hearing those words from Sammi Jo.

Not ready to examine why, he turned to his tried-and-true distraction.

"Then let's see what kind of dream we can come up with this time," he suggested.

He shifted Sammi on top of him, his hands guiding her into position. Her eyes were bright, all that wild red hair tousled around a face flushed with desire and whisker burns. Her smile filled with sweet desire.

And for the first time in his life, he worried about being as good as a woman deserved.

10

MMM. SHE FELT so good.

Had she ever felt this good?

Wrapped in the warmth of Laramie's arms and an amazing dream, Sammi Jo drifted in that magical place between sleeping and awake, snuggling deeper into the delight.

She breathed deep, her entire being filled with Laramie's scent. His touch. His flavor. And last night, his body. God, he was amazing. Her fingers curled into the scattering of hair on Laramie's chest while her mind tallied the orgasms. Yes, she'd had more orgasms in the past thirty-six hours than she'd had in her entire life. Even now, teetering on the edge of exhaustion, her body was so tender with pleasure that even breathing was a turn-on.

She lay there listening to his heartbeat, for the first time understanding the obsession so many people had with sex. She hated thinking about next week when the sex would be gone. Laramie would be gone.

Laramie would be gone, and she'd be facing the fallout of cancelling her wedding. Oh, how ugly it would be.

It was the right thing to do, though. Now that she knew what happy really felt like, could she settle for less? She'd have to, she realized. Because, again, Laramie was leaving in a week.

And taking all the great sex, and happiness, with him.

Tension grabbed tight, squeezing away the pleasure until all that was left was burning eyes and a knot of misery in her belly. Sammi struggled to breathe through the panic. Now, instead of combing her fingers through Laramie's chest hair she was grabbing enough to yank it all out.

Afraid of waking him, even more afraid of having to try to explain the flurry of emotions to him before she even understood them herself, Sammi carefully slipped off his body and, with enough regret to make her eyes burn again, climbed out of the bed.

The hardwood feeling like ice against her bare feet, Sammi froze, her eyes locked on Laramie's face until she was sure she hadn't woke him. She counted to ten, timing her count to his inhalations. Then she counted another ten, because well, look at that gorgeous chest. When her fingers tingled with the need to touch him again, she forced herself to hurry from the room.

In the tiny bathroom, Sammi pressed her hands against her chest, hoping the odd feeling in there was illness, not her heart breaking. Peering into the black-splotched mirror, she studied her face. Messy morning hair tangled in a halo around her pale face. Her eyes were blurry and faintly bruised from her lack of sleep and her lips a little swollen. But all in all, she looked like herself.

By the time she was sitting in the rickety rocker on the porch with her coffee, Sammi was laughing at herself. Silly, being scared of awesome sex. Just because wild physical encounters and multiple orgasms weren't normal in her world didn't mean she couldn't enjoy them.

For now.

But even as the thought occurred to her, Sammi realized that it wasn't the awesome sex that she was afraid of.

It was what it meant for the rest of her life that scared the bejesus out of her.

She'd been so wrapped up in Laramie, so focused on the two of them and how good she felt with him, that she'd conveniently ignored reality.

Even as they'd made love a third time in the shower that first night, turning each other on as they washed away the stickiness of their frosting-coated sex, she hadn't been worried. After all, it was just the two of them.

Because they'd wanted to keep it just the two of them, they'd snuck out of her apartment in the wee hours. Sammi hadn't thought twice at Laramie's suggestion that she follow him in her truck so that nobody questioned her not being at the inn.

They'd spent the past few days at the cabin exploring a kaleidoscope of delights. Sex and laughter. Shared secrets and mutual orgasms. Long looks and satisfied moans. They'd talked about everything from memories to movies, pastimes to politics. He'd told her a little about his job. Not the secret stuff, but the type of training that went into it. She'd told him about her work at the inn and the frustration of feeling stuck.

But now, with the bright morning sun burning through the fantasy she'd wrapped herself in, she had to face reality.

Wild physical encounters and multiple orgasms shouldn't be a part of her life because she was engaged to be married.

Sammi took a careful sip of her coffee, hoping the flavor would wash away the bitterness in her throat.

That she'd been okay with that before—so okay with it that she'd defended the idea of spending her life in a blandly sexless, humorless, joyless marriage—proved how messed up her thinking was.

Or maybe just how messed up her life would be if she actually married Sterling.

There.

She'd admitted it.

Her engagement was a mistake and she wanted out of it.

How did she get out of it, though?

The wedding was in a week and a half. She had two dresses, four bridesmaids, a bland white cake without iced cherry frosting and a father-of-the-groom with very specific expectations.

And a missing fiancé.

Who'd been thoughtful enough to text the previous night to assure her that he was okay—and to ask her to make sure his rent was paid on time. Since Laramie had insisted she text back with questions only Sterling could answer as what he called *proof of life*, she felt pretty confident believing that he really was okay.

And, given that nowhere in his texts had he expressed any affection or assurances, she felt just as confident believing that she wouldn't be breaking his heart when she ended the engagement. His father, of course, was a different matter altogether.

But while she was grateful to Mr. Barclay, she realized that Laramie was right. She'd let the older man run her life. Right down to taking his subtle hints to marry his son, she realized with a surprised shake of her head.

Well, no more.

She couldn't break it off with Sterling until she talked with him face-to-face. Until then, she was going to embrace the moment and enjoy every second of her time with Laramie.

Her head resting on the chair, Sammi closed her eyes

and rocked. Despite knowing that the next week would be filled with arguments, pressure, gossip and finger-pointing judgment, she felt a deep sense of inner calm. She breathed in the rich fragrance of her coffee mingling with the clear mountain air and realized that whatever else happened, now that she'd made the decision to break it off with Sterling, she was at peace.

Ten minutes later, wrapped in a gray checked shirt so big it could wrap around her twice and with her smile finally at ease, Sammi Jo hummed her way into the kitchen. Her bare feet made no sound on the sun-dappled hardwood floor, but the refrigerator door squealed a protest as she pulled it open.

No wonder, she noted with raised brows. The poor thing was practically empty. She considered the shelf of beer cans, two eggs and a hunk of salami, then shrugged.

Who said a person couldn't live on love?

Sammi gave a little shiver of delight, reveling in the freedom of being able to do whatever she wanted. And, she ran a hand down her well-pleasured body, whoever she wanted.

And what she wanted right now was breakfast. Who cared if the pickings were slim? She would make something awesome, anyway.

Humming again, she grabbed the eggs and salami before moving to the tiny square that was the only counter space. She started a search through the cabinets. She'd slice the salami thin to fry it up like bacon and scramble the eggs. Along the way, she found a loaf of bread, two apples and a jar of peanut butter.

Slicing the salami, she couldn't help but smile at the idea of Laramie being a PB&J guy. She'd have pegged him a red-meat-lovin' chili eater, but discovering all these sweet little details about him was just one reason why she was fascinated.

Sammi jumped when two large hands slipped around her waist, her yelp of shock ricocheting around the room.

How did he move like that? She should have heard him, shouldn't she? The cabin was silent but for the birds outside and the faint hum of the ancient refrigerator.

"I was just making something for breakfast," she said, her words breathless. Shouldn't she feel shy with him? Or at least a smidge uncomfortable?

His hands found bare flesh, leaving trails of heat as they skimmed over her belly. Sammi shot a look out the curtainless window, checking for the deer. When she noted that the brush outside appeared wildlife-free, she relaxed back into Laramie's chest and sighed her pleasure.

"I'm not hungry for food," he said, nuzzling her hair aside so he could nibble on her throat. His hands cupped her breasts, squeezing rhythmically while his fingers gently twisted her nipples into fiery need.

"Don't you need fuel to keep your energy up?" Sammi asked, her words a breathless gasp as she tossed the food aside to grip the countertop so she didn't fall.

"Sugar, after the last two days, how can you doubt my ability to keep it up?" His laughter was a soft caress over her tingling skin, his body tight against hers.

The feel of his erection pressing against her just below the curve of her spine made her tremble. They'd had each other so many times, in so many ways. Yet just the feel of him had her instantly wet and needy.

She tried to turn. She wanted him now. She needed the long, hard length of him inside her. But instead of letting her, his hands tightened so that his fingers bit into her breasts. Sammi gasped, need coiling tight between her thighs.

"Laramie."

He shifted his hands, one banding across her body so he still held her trapped while his fingers teased her nipple. The other slid down her torso, through her Brazilian curls and over her hot, wet core. He dipped a testing finger inside, then before she could do more than moan, he grabbed her waist and lifted so her belly was pressed against the narrow counter. Both hands caressed their way up her hips, lifting her shirt high and angling her just so before he slid inside her from behind.

"Oh, God," she breathed, her body welcoming his, wrapping around him like a tight glove. Even as she reveled in the erotic delight of being taken from behind, of being bent over a countertop, hot flames of desire engulfed her. He was so deep he was a part of her.

His hands cupped her breasts. He thrust again and again until Sammi cried out with the pleasure pouring through her. Her climax came in a flash, light exploding behind her eyes. Before she could catch her breath, she felt his orgasm rock through her body, sending her over again. This time with enough intensity that everything behind her eyes went black. When Sammi came back to awareness, she was still tingling and Laramie's body was resting against hers.

As she took a shaky breath, he murmured, "Good morning, sugar."

HIKING TO THE TOP of his favorite trail, Laramie breathed deep the peace as if he could store it inside and take it with him when he left.

This was why he came back each year, he realized.

"It's so beautiful here."

He glanced over at Sammi's soft murmur, surprised at how perfect she looked sitting in his thinking spot. Her ponytailed hair gilded in the sunset and dark glasses shading her eyes, she'd wrapped her arms around her knees and rested her chin there to look out over the valley below.

She gave him peace, he realized with a frown. Or maybe it was contentment. He'd never experienced it before, so he couldn't be sure. The past few days had been filled with her. They'd made love and talked. They'd slept and ate and showered and made love some more. And talked. He wasn't sure what it was about her, or if it was something about them since she seemed surprised at how much she'd confessed, too. Whatever it was, it was rare and it was special.

And he wasn't sure he wanted to let it go.

"It must make it easier to leave each year knowing that this will be here when you get back." Sammi gestured to the view, the tans, reds and greens beyond the valley blurring together like a watercolor. "It's as if it hasn't changed in hundreds of years."

"I used to come here a lot when I was a kid," he confessed, taking her hand in his to rub each finger in turn. "When I was upset or pissed, or just wanted some space from my parents' fighting. I could think here."

"Your mom always seemed like a sea of calm to me." Sammi cringed and pressed her fingers to her lips as if wishing she could shove the words back in. "I'm sorry. I know you don't like to talk about her."

Nope. He didn't.

But even as Laramie felt himself closing in, wrapping his heart tightly around the memories, Sammi rose from the log, stepped over and took his hand.

"It's a great thinking place," she said with an understanding smile. "The vastness seems as if it'd put problems into perspective, and the quiet offers little in the way of distractions."

As a change of subject, it was about as obvious as it was

sweet. He meshed their fingers together, then led her back to the log where he pulled her onto his lap. With Sammi's head resting on his shoulder, he stared out at the valley.

"She was calm, most of the time. She liked to sing when she worked and she made friends easy. Wherever we were on the rodeo circuit, she'd gather women around her and make us a home. She never raised her voice to me. She didn't have to. She'd get this look in her eyes and just shake her head, and I swear, that was as much a punishment as getting my butt walloped by my father. But they fought a lot. When he died, I figured it'd get easier."

Laramie rested his head on the silky softness of Sammi's hair, the view blurring at the edges as he remembered.

"I was tired of living at my uncle's, wanted to get on with our lives, so I bugged her to move home. To me, the cabin was always home." Memories poured through him, hard, fast and painfully clear. "She was sick. She thought it was just a summer cold, you know how those hang on. Then she got worse. I couldn't drive. Was always on a horse at that age, so I'd had no interest in learning to operate a vehicle. I wouldn't have left her, anyway—she was getting so bad. I did what I could, but it didn't help. Next thing I knew, she was gone."

Meningitis. It had taken her from him so damned fast.

"She loved you, Christian. That was obvious to anyone who saw the two of you together, or heard her talk about you. She'd be proud of you. Not only for what you've become, but for what you've overcome."

Laramie gave a half shrug. He didn't figure she'd be ashamed.

Sammi shifted so she could see his face. Her eyes serious, she laid her hand on his cheek.

"I didn't know her well, but I know her through you. And through the things people say." She paused, as if waiting for him to understand how thorough and well-informed the gossip chain was. "I think it would hurt her to think that you were still blaming yourself for her dying."

That his choices, his actions had caused her pain was a guilt he would carry his entire life. But for the first time since he'd seen his mother fall to the floor, the heaviness of blame lifted. Not completely. But enough to let in a few other memories. Warm, happy memories.

He sighed and started to thank Sammi Jo. Instead, he found himself leaning down to take her mouth with his.

There was no lust in the kiss. The goal wasn't sex. As their lips slid together, it was joy and friendship that filled his body. It was the simple peace of knowing he was with someone who made him feel like the best person he could be. Someone who filled him with a self-acceptance that he'd never felt before.

"Wow," Sammi breathed the word again, her eyes huge and, this time, blurry with desire. "Was that a thank-you?"

"That. And it was because I like you," he said slowly.

It was as simple, and as complicated, as that.

"Have you ever thought about leaving Jerrick?" he heard himself ask. At Sammi's shocked stare, he shrugged. "If Barclay decides to move or something. Would you leave?"

She bit her lip, then as if talking about her fiancé while sitting on another man's lap bugged her, she slid down to sit on the log next to him.

"I don't know. I can't imagine living anywhere else." She shrugged. "Even after you talked me out of running away, I used to dream about leaving. I wanted to see places, explore the world, just get out of Texas. But then things changed."

"Where did you want to explore?" Anyplace he might be assigned?

"I wanted to swim in every ocean, to visit other countries. I wanted to fly in an airplane and see snow on the mountains." Her words dreamy, Sammi snuggled closer to rest her head on the crook of his shoulder.

"So why aren't you?"

"Working at the inn doesn't offer a lot of opportunity to travel," she pointed out, her smile fading as fast as it came, leaving a tiny line creasing her brow.

"Is the inn where you want to be working? Is that the career you chose? When we were kids, you used to talk about doing something artistic."

"I actually made pretty decent money painting cards and stuff when I was in college. I developed this style that went over really well and had so much fun doing it."

Her face lit up as she described the various techniques she'd used for different messages. He had no idea what bokeh was, and wet-on-wet sounded kinky as hell. He did like the way her face lit up and how animated her gestures were as she described it.

"You're still making this line of cards and stationary, right?" He'd get some and write to her from wherever he was stationed. She'd probably get a kick out of seeing her own card arrive from Kabul or Germany.

"Not really. I mean, I make a few things here and there as gifts for friends, but I gave up on the idea of art for a living years ago. There's no way I could actually support myself with my little drawings and paint splatters," she said, the words so matter-of-factly automatic that Laramie wondered who'd made them her reality.

Whoever it was, he had the urge to punch them. She shouldn't be giving up her dreams.

"You sound more excited about that than anything I've heard you say about running the inn. Sounds to me as if that's a better direction for you than what you're doing now."

Her face lit as if he'd just paid her a huge compliment, then fell just as fast.

"Maybe, but it takes a lot to start a new career. By the time I'd have enough inventory to make it doable, I'd be way too old," she laughed.

Where the hell was she getting this stuff? Sammi Jo was only twenty-four. He knew guys who went to school, started new careers in their forties. They left the military and started from scratch.

"You know, I have a friend who runs an art gallery. Mostly ceramics and glass, but they have this little gift shop and I think everything there is handmade, too."

"Mmm, would this be a lady friend?" Sammi asked with an eye roll.

"Sure, but not like that. She's married to one of my teammates," he said, thinking of Lark and Shane. "She's got a lot of contacts in the art world. I'm sure she'd like to take a look at your cards. She can tell you what it'd take to get started."

"You'd do that? You'd ask your friend's wife to help me out?"

Laramie frowned, not sure why she sounded so shocked. "Of course."

"You are the sweetest man I've ever known," she said, rubbing her lips over his before curling into his arms.

That wasn't an answer, but Laramie figured that meant a *yes* was still possible. He'd just have to work up to getting her to agree, that's all.

And he didn't know about being the sweetest man. But he felt whole when he was with Sammi. As if the pieces of his world that had been broken for so long had finally mended. For a man whose life was filled with epic choices and life-or-death scenarios, it was a huge thing. What would it be like to have this feeling all the time?

Laramie remembered his first free-fall jump from a helicopter into the storm-raged Pacific. He'd stood on the edge of the bay door of a mechanically sound Chinook, staring into the icy, black walls below. And he'd known that with one step, he could be plummeting to a viciously painful death or he could be proving that he was worthy of the Trident he'd worked so hard to earn. Either way, he'd figured he'd never be the same again.

Staring into Sammi Jo's pretty face, he felt exactly the same as he had standing on the edge of that bay door. If his emotions shifted another inch closer to that precipice, it would either change his life.

Or break his heart.

11

CELL PHONE TO his ear, Laramie sat on the railing outside the Packing District, rolling his eyes at the bar that proudly advertised its meat-market status on a neon sign flashing from blue to red and back again.

As if anyone could miss it otherwise?

The place was doing big business tonight, and not just because of Sammi Jo's bachelorette party. The parking lot was jammed tight and sounds rolled out of the building like thunder each time the wide entry door opened.

"Genius said to tell you he's tapped into the business partner. You were right. There's something shady going on with that guy," Taylor was saying in Laramie's ear. "So what's going on at your end? Were you able to deploy Operation Rich Boy Rescue without us? You get that dumbass back yet?"

"Once I'd determined that he wasn't in actual danger, I scaled back my efforts. He and the partner are up to something." That or Barclay really was a dumbass. Laramie shook his head, figuring nobody could be that stupid. "The dumbass actually called Sammi this morning to remind her to check his PO box for some training program he'd ordered."

"Dude's been kidnapped. Maybe that was some sort of code. Maybe coordinates to his location or encrypted details on who the kidnappers are."

Laramie gave a derisive snort.

"That'd be a no." Then, because it was Taylor, he admitted, "I checked."

"Huh. So he really is a dumbass."

They took a moment to ponder the stupidity of some people before Taylor changed the subject.

"So when are we going to meet the woman who has you all but hog-tied and branded?" On the other end of the line, Taylor deliberately hesitated. "That's the cowboy way of saying that you're gaga over your Texas sweetheart, right?"

"I'm not gaga, and I'll never be hog-tied and branded," Laramie said dismissively, his shoulders twitching uncomfortably.

"Yeah, fine. Whatever. So when do we get to meet her?" Taylor said with a laugh.

"Probably around three days after never."

Not because he wanted to keep her secret. Hell, he'd already talked to Lark about her, had sent her a package with the handful of cards and stationary he'd been able to charm away from Sammi. Picturing Sammi Jo in San Diego was pure pleasure. She'd love the beaches and she'd fit right in with the team's ladies. His friends would welcome her into their circle because she was with him. But as soon as they got to know her, they'd want her there for herself.

The question was, would she go?

And what if she didn't?

He stared unseeingly at the parking lot, mentally picturing how that'd play out. Would she visit when he was on leave? Or just a weekend here and there, and he'd spend leave here? Most of the team lived in Southern California. It was just easier that way. But a few had a family that hadn't moved to California when they transferred. He'd always felt sorry for those guys, spending most of their leave traveling, then mowing lawns or some damned thing. Now he wondered how they pulled it off.

"Yo, Wizard." Laramie hesitated. Then, needing to know, more than he wanted to pretend he didn't care, he asked, "How do you do it? How do you make it work?"

In the typical way of the team, Taylor instantly understood the question without Laramie having to elaborate.

"Me and Cat?" The other man was silent for a moment. "We just do. It helps that we were friends before we got together, but I don't think that'd matter in the grand scheme of things."

Laramie knew that Taylor and his fiancée had grown up on the same street. Their moms were even best friends. Laramie didn't figure that would have been a possibility even if his mom had been alive, but he figured having a friendship that went back to grade school days would work well enough.

"What about when you're deployed? You, Romeo, Scavenger, you all seem to roll with it. I don't see you getting stressed about being away from your women for weeks, months at a time. But don't they get pissed?"

"Pissed? Why?" His words genuinely surprised, Taylor dismissed that with an airy *pshaw*. "Look, dude, we were all on the team when we got together with our women. They knew the score before signing on. And, I don't know, I guess we'd all served long enough to know how to handle it right."

Laramie didn't need his friend to elaborate. They'd both seen plenty of guys who'd joined the SEALs thinking they knew what they were facing, then washing right back out. It took a special kind of strength to actually make it in the SEALs, a strength that didn't always appear right away.

Some guys took years to figure out how to balance the demands of their career, their commitment to the team and actually have a life, too.

"Bottom line, Cowboy, is if you want something, you make it happen. If it matters, you make it happen right."

Laramie blew out a breath, wishing he could expel the nagging doubts as easily. Or, better yet, he'd like to ditch the insane thoughts about making a long-distance… thing—he couldn't quite wrap his mind around the word *relationship*—work. Yeah, he knew it was crazy to think that there was a way to make a long-distance thing work between him and Sammi Jo.

But the alternative was not seeing her again.

Ending the call with their usual volley of insults, Laramie walked into the bar, still pondering the idea of life without Sammi Jo. No matter how he maneuvered the images in his head, he didn't like the way it looked.

As he wended his way through the bodies, he turned down two offers to dance, one for something a little more intimate, ignored the pats on his ass and offered a deadly stare to a cowboy who looked as if he was going to start a fight.

Leave it to Blythe Horton to pick a place like this to throw her best friend a bachelorette party. Three floors of space dedicated to getting drunk and hooking up, the floors were cement, the booths were Naugahyde and each floor boasted a horseshoe-shaped bar. The noise level on the first floor was loud but not quite loud enough to drown out the painfully twanging chords of the band upstairs. Upstairs or down, the name of the game was grab-ass, cowboy style. Boots and hats were the only consistent part of the dress code, with women in cutoff shorts and others in dresses, a few sporting overalls and others in slacks.

Laramie ran his hand over his bare head, feeling a little

exposed without his own hat. His gaze scanned the crowd until he found it, then commandeered a booth with a view of the mechanical bull just in time to watch Sammi Jo step up to the motorized beast.

He smiled at the look of nervous determination on her face as she carefully removed his hat and hung it from the peg next to the bull. She smoothed a hand over her wavy hair, then wiped both hands on her jeans, lifted her chin and mounted the beast.

She took a deep breath. For a second he thought she was going to be sick, then she took another, deeper breath. Then, one hand in the air, she nodded.

Laramie's grin widened.

Damned if she wasn't something. Desire and pride mixed it up in his belly as she handled the bull as if she'd done it a dozen times before. He couldn't wait to tease her about hitting the rodeo circuit.

Her body swayed gracefully, swinging to the left and then to the right. Her hair flew around her head in a deep russet halo. But his eyes were fixed on her breasts as they bounced in time with the motion of the bull.

She looked like that when she straddled him. The same focused concentration on her face, the same deliciously tempting moves of her body.

As she finished her ride to a cacophony of cheers and catcalls, Laramie readily acknowledged that he wanted her like he'd never wanted anyone else. But watching her now he had to admit that want was only the tip of an iceberg called need. And the need, he was pretty sure, was grounded in love.

Damn it all to hell.

"Well, well, lookie who graced our little town."

His body tensing even more, his senses on full alert,

Laramie simply glanced to the left and arched his brow when an older woman slid into the booth opposite him.

"You keep watching my little girl like that, people are gonna talk." Cora Mae tapped an unlit cigarette on the table between them as she tossed back what looked like whiskey.

From the deep wrinkles around her eyes to the silver roots of her long blond hair, the woman had aged. She was so skinny that her ribs were visible beneath the tight black T tucked into a skirt no longer than the span of a man's hand. Her scrawny legs were crossed beneath that swatch of denim, the harsh bar lights emphasizing every inch of craggy cellulite. Red nail polish matched the backless stiletto dangling from her toes as she swung her foot to and fro.

Under kinder lighting, her face might be attractive. She had the same big green eyes and full-lipped overbite as her daughter; time had not been kind to the older woman.

"You're looking for Sterling Barclay," she stated, her cigarette-roughened words barely above a whisper and the urgent tone at odds with her bored expression. "What's it worth for a little help finding him?"

Laramie didn't say a word. He simply leaned back, letting his arm rest along the back of the chair. And waited.

The simple intimidation tactic worked quicker than he'd expected.

"Look, this new guy dropped by my trailer a couple nights ago. He got a little drunk and let it slip that he and his buddy gonna be rolling in the dough and all they have to do is sit on some rich schmuck for a couple of weeks."

"Barclay?"

"It's not like he named names." Cora Mae's sneer didn't have a chance against Laramie's steely stare.

"He said the guy was a local and that he was figuring

on getting a new car out of the deal." She shrugged one bony shoulder as if to say who else could it be?

Laramie simply waited. The woman tried to wait him out, but after a handful of seconds, her face tightened. She huffed, her hand fisting at her side.

"Fine. So maybe he thought it was funny that they were holding him on property the guy played on as a kid."

Some of the tension leaving his shoulders, Laramie considered her words. No question that Cora Mae would likely run with the types of losers involved in kidnapping a dumbass like Barclay. Those types tended to be stupid.

The only part he wasn't buying was that she'd put any effort into helping her daughter. That she'd put out effort and take a risk? That stepped over the line from doubtful to impossible.

Still…

"How about you tell me the rest," he suggested quietly, finally unbending enough to take a drink of his beer.

Cora Mae poked out her bottom lip on a move surprisingly like her daughter before sighing.

"After a few drinks he started bragging about how he was gonna be making double what he'd haul on any other job because the whole thing was a setup."

Laramie gave a ghost of a nod. That jibed with the info Mr. Wizard had mentioned.

"I made a joke about him leaving the country after it was over, you know, cuz the rich guy had seen his face." Cora leaned closer, hunching her shoulders so she looked a little like a blonde vulture. "He patted his gun and said rich boy talking wasn't gonna be a problem."

Laramie's spine stiffened at the ominous insinuation. Now that was new information.

Still…

"Why are you telling me this?"

She rocked, leaned back in her seat. Just for a second, her gaze shifted toward Sammi Jo's side of the bar, then she gave Laramie a bored look and shrugged.

"Word is you've got the skills to find rich boy."

Laramie inclined his head.

"And if I don't want to?"

She slammed her glass down with enough force that the ice cubes bounced. She glanced to the left, then to the right before hissing the words across the table.

"You need to back off Sammi Jo before you ruin her reputation. If word gets out that you've been hanging around, she's gonna lose everything. Her rich husband, her fancy-ass job, all of it."

"Like you give a damn?" Laramie asked with a sardonic laugh.

Cora Mae's eyes shifted across the bar toward the laughing knot of women surrounding her daughter. For a brief moment her expression folded into something that looked like regret, then she shrugged it off with the same ease she'd shrugged off everything else about her only child.

"What difference does it make if I give a damn or not?" She swirled her glass, what was left of her whiskey sloshing over the clanking ice cubes. "Bottom line is you're going to screw up her life if you keep horndogging around here. You think she's gonna throw over rich boy for you?"

She gave him a cynical once over, then arched one penciled-on eyebrow.

"Maybe she will. But you are going to take off soon enough. What do you think's gonna happen then? What do you think Sammi's going to do? Sit around waiting for your yearly visit?" Cora Mae's snort of a laugh made it clear that she figured the answer was a resounding *Hell, no.* Elbowing her glass of melting ice aside, she planted her forearms on the table and leaned forward until she was right in Laramie's face. "Word about the two of you is going to ruin her rep. That girl doesn't deserve to have her life ruined like that."

"Word about her being involved with me would ruin her life?" Even as Laramie rolled his eyes, Cora Mae was nodding so hard a long hank of blond hair landed in her glass.

"You think that old butt pirate, Barclay, is going to let her keep her job when he hears about the two of you? You think he's gonna let her live in that dump of a garage he stuck her in?" Cora Mae snorted. "That jackass pays her a chump change, so it's not like she's got a fat savings account to fall back on. And you know he'll give the beady eye to anyone who even thinks about hiring her. So what's Sammi Jo gonna do then, smart guy?"

Taking in those truths and new realizations, Laramie lowered his gaze to his beer bottle and frowned. He hadn't realized how tight a hold old man Barclay had on Sammi Jo's life.

Then again, he had to consider the source.

Laramie speared Cora Mae with sharp look as she slid out of her seat.

"Why?" At her blank look, he expanded. "Why the tip? Why the warning? Why'd you bother?"

The look that flashed over the older woman's face was all the answer he needed. Vulnerable pain and quickly masked loss said that no matter how lousy a mother—or human being—she was, she cared about Sammi Jo.

But Cora Mae being Cora Mae, she quickly buried that redeeming emotion with a sneer. She cocked her bony hip to one side and gave him a hard look.

"You screw up her life bad enough, she's going to end up having to move back in with me. And there just ain't room enough in my trailer for two women." She slapped her hand on her hip and gave him an arch look. "So don't you go messing up my life just because you can't keep your dick in your pants."

With that and a practiced toss of her hair, Cora Mae gave her shoulders a little wiggle and slid right back into the hard-edged bitch she'd always been. She pressed her hands onto the tabletop and bent down, the move leaving her shirt gaping enough to show Laramie and every man behind him that her bra matched her high heels.

"Sammi Jo is rooted here. She's got a chance at a better life than I could have ever gave her. So you do right by her, hotshot. You do right and get the hell out of her life."

With that and another toss of her smoke-scented hair, Cora Mae sauntered out of the bar. Leaving Laramie feeling like he'd just been kicked in the balls.

"Go, baby, go!"

Waving the hat she'd claimed as her own in the air, Sammi Jo cheered as Clara showed that mechanical bull who was boss.

Was it okay to have this much fun at a bachelorette party when she intended to stay a bachelorette? Sammi Jo had no clue, and thanks to her second margarita, she didn't care. She was simply loving every second of doing what felt good.

Dancing with her girlfriends without worrying about looking stupid.

Riding a mechanical bull without caring that it wasn't ladylike.

And best of all, Sammi decided as she settled her jean-clad butt onto a bar stool, wearing a man's hat in public as if it were her own, especially when the man was notorious for his bad cowboy ways. Not that she expected anyone to actually recognize Laramie's Stetson. Nine out of ten men in town wore similar hats.

But she knew.

It felt so sexy. Just as the fact that Laramie was here in the bar, somewhere, waiting to take her back to his cabin later felt sexy. She shifted on the stool, trying to find a position that didn't challenge thighs made sore from riding the bull—and Laramie.

"Sammi Jo, you're glowing with so damned much happiness, you're gonna blind us all." Blythe sidled up to the bar, bumping her shoulder against Sammi's. "Everybody's talking about it. They're saying you're acting mighty happy."

"Don't most brides-to-be glow?" Sammi asked, surreptitiously looking around to see who might be doing the talking and wishing she didn't care so much.

"Sure they do. They glow a little brighter when the hottest guy to ever grace our town is staring at the bride-to-be as if he were the big bad wolf and she was about to get eaten."

Sammi's lips twitched as she wondered how Laramie would like being compared to the big bad wolf.

"Be careful," Blythe added in a low whisper. Her expression was festive, but Sammi could see the worry in her eyes. "They're gonna remember because this is the first time he's set foot in this bar, added to the first time you've been here. Throw in those hot stares and you breaking off your engagement and the gossips are gonna have a heyday."

"I can't live my life worrying about what people are going to say," Sammi decided.

"Your lust for Laramie is going to get you into trouble if you're not careful," Blythe warned before heeding the call that it was her turn on the bull.

It wasn't just lust, Sammy mentally corrected as her friend hurried away.

She felt a lot more than that for Laramie. Fascination and delight. She was attracted to his mind and his strength as much as she was to his body. She admired his dedication and his focus on being the best.

And maybe was in love with him.

But what did she know about love?

What if this was just infatuation instead?

And even if it was love, what if it didn't last?

Blythe's words, sparked by Sammi's own fears, flamed hot with the nerves in her belly. Maybe she just needed some ice water, something to cool those nerves and her thoughts.

Before she could wave over the bartender, a hand skimmed down her back.

"Laramie?" she exclaimed, twisting in her seat to give him a horrified look. "What are you doing?"

"Asking you to dance," he gestured toward the corner where the music was loudest and people were boot scooting. "How about it?"

"You're supposed to be staying away from me," she hissed, peering over his shoulder, trying to see through the crowd to make sure Blythe wasn't coming back with another lecture.

"Its just a dance, Sammi Jo. I wasn't going to strip you naked and show the crowd what you look like riding me instead of that bull."

"Don't say things like that. Not in here." Color washed her cheeks as, shoulders hunched, she looked left, then right. Then behind her for good measure.

"So what's the deal? Are you ashamed of me?"

"No, but I have to live here, remember."

Laramie's expression barely changed, but a chill ran down Sammi's back, making her shiver.

"You've got plenty of girlfriends here, right?" he asked in a neutral tone.

Not sure why she felt a sudden foreboding, Sammi didn't take her eyes off him as she nodded.

"Catch a ride home with one who hasn't been drinking, okay? I've got to go."

Before she could ask where, before she could even respond, he turned on the heel of his cowboy boot and disappeared into the crowd.

"Whoa, wait."

Sammi slid off the stool and hurried through the wall of bodies, chasing after him. The clashing scents of perfume, cologne and booze made her head spin a little, so that she gratefully sucked in gulps of fresh air the minute she hit the door.

There was a crowd out here, too, milling between the outdoor tables, leaning against the railroad tie fence. But at least here, she could breathe.

"Wait," she called again, not caring who saw her as she hurried to catch Laramie before he hit the parking lot. "Just hold up a damned second."

It must have been the *damn* that did it, because he not only slowed, he stopped, turned and faced her with that same blank expression.

"Aren't you worried about what people are gonna say, seeing you chase me down like this?"

"Why are you acting like this?" She threw her hands in the air before planting them on her jean-clad hips. "What is wrong with you?"

"I heard something that didn't sit right with me."

"What?" What could have him acting so cold and unreasonable?

He wasn't saying, though. Instead he looked back toward the bar, then at her.

"What about your reputation? You want it getting back to the Barclays that you've been seen with me?"

Yes. But she was afraid telling him that would just make him angrier.

"I think that it'd be wrong to sashay around, flaunting the fact that I'm with someone else before I have a chance to tell Sterling myself," she said carefully. "And I think that's the sort of thing I need to tell him face-to-face."

"Right. But it's okay if everyone knows that he's screwing around on you as long as you're not kidnapped?"

As shocked as if he'd shoved her on her butt, Sammi could only shake her head as she tried to catch her breath.

"Why are you doing this? Why are you being so ugly all of a sudden?"

Laramie raked his hand over his head, closed his eyes and sighed.

"Its hard, okay. It's hard realizing that I'm breaking my own rule with you and having an affair with a woman committed to someone else. So committed," he said before she could respond, "that despite whatever has happened between us, she's going to marry someone else."

Ohhh. Awareness poured through her, quickly followed by relief. Her stomach unknotted enough that Sammi was able to smile.

"I'm ending my engagement," she said quietly, ignoring the stares probing her back like lasers and reaching out to take Laramie's hand. "I thought you realized that. I thought you knew."

"You're not going to marry Barclay?"

"No," she said with a relieved laugh. Whew. Now everything could be okay again.

"Then leave. Let Barclay deal with his own mess. Come with me to San Diego."

Seriously?

Sammi's head spun. She wanted to. Oh, how she wanted to. She felt as if her heart was exploding in her chest, filled with too much joy to contain. But her stomach was so tight with worries, her head so full of doubts, that she couldn't feel the joy. How would she support herself? What would she do? She'd be leaving her job, her home, all her friends. But was he asking because he liked the sex? Did he mean he wanted her to live there or to just visit for a while? Would they live together or was he thinking a hotel room for a weekend?

"I can't," she heard herself say, the words sounding like they'd been forced through a long tunnel. "Not right now. Not like this."

If he loved her, she'd go. If he loved her, she'd follow him to the ends of the earth and back. She wanted to ask Laramie why he wanted her, what he felt for her. She wanted to push him to confess his feelings, to explain what he was really asking.

But a lifetime of rejection kept her lips closed tight and her heart aching with the anticipation of pain.

"And after Barclay is back? After right now is done?" Then, before she could respond, before she could even think of how to answer, he shook his head. "Forget I said that. Just forget all of it."

"I'm sorry." All of her fears, all of her excuses trembled on the tip of her tongue. But Sammi could only shake her head. "What we've had, it means so much to me. But I can't just walk way. I'm not trying to be ungrateful—"

He shook his head, stopping her words cold.

His eyes chilled to ice.

"We had a good time." He shrugged. "Consider your debt paid in full, sugar."

He turned and walked away.

It took her until he'd reached his truck to find her voice.

"Where are you going?" she called, forgetting—not caring about—their audience.

"To bring you back your fucking fiancé."

MAYBE IT WAS a questionable decision to take a late-night horseback ride into the den of armed kidnappers on the word of a half-drunk tramp.

But given that his only other option was hauling Sammi Jo out of that damned bar and sharing his feelings, Laramie had saddled up his horse.

Now, guiding Star along the moonlit path toward a cabin that, according to Art, had once belonged to the Barclays on the north side of Cone Peak, with the wind cooling his skin and the freedom of open land all around, he enjoyed the ride.

He could have driven in, but this was four-wheel drive terrain and he wanted to keep his approach silent. He figured the extraction would be quick and easy. He had rope, a flashlight and water in his saddlebag. He hadn't bothered with a weapon, figuring that'd be overkill. And since he didn't plan on riding double, the truck and trailer were waiting about a mile away.

When he was a quarter mile from the cabin he swung off Star, loosely tethering the gelding to a tree by the trickling stream. All he needed for the initial recon was the flashlight, so he tucked that into the pocket of his denim jacket and hooked his hat on a low-hanging branch. He gave the horse a pat on the flank, then headed up the hill.

The cabin was surrounded by tall bushes, a copse of summer-browned trees and dirt. A lot of dirt. Laramie crouched behind a stunted piñon, rubbing his hands into that dirt, then transferring it to his face while he assessed the situation.

Two guys stood beside a beat-up Jeep with out-of-state

plates. Each with a pistol on their hip. Keeping low, Laramie angled toward the cabin. It had windows on all four sides and from the dimensions it looked like two rooms. Heading for the unlit side, he checked the back window. A cot, a chair and two doors, one open to the head. Through the other, he could see nothing more than a brightly lit room. No bodies.

Needing to ascertain that Barclay was here before he took out the guards, he dropped to a crouch, moving toward the east side of the building.

After figuring out that he only heard a single voice, Laramie shifted to the side so he could see through the window.

Like the other, this room was sparsely furnished. A card table and two chairs. A minifridge with a microwave on top and a beat-up TV/DVD combo.

And a cot, with Barclay kicked back on it like a guy without a care in the world. His back propped against the wall, loafer-clad feet crossed at the ankles, the guy was chatting away on his cell phone.

Laramie leaned closer to the window, listening. Then almost growled as enough of the other man's words filtered through to realize that Barclay was talking to his girlfriend.

Laramie wanted to pound on the asshole, then reminded himself the dumbass would eventually pay the price for being such a pathetic example of humanity. They always did one way or the other.

But watching the jerk make kissy noises into the phone made it damned hard to depend on eventually.

Fueled by fury, Laramie ignored stealth, simply striding toward the front of the building. Before the goons could react, he grabbed the bigger of the two and with a quick flip sent him flying. Momentum carried his fist into the other man's jaw, sending him toppling backward over the jeep.

Laramie stood there, fists tightened, waiting for one of them to move. But they were both out cold.

Dammit.

He took a minute to remove their weapons and disable the Jeep before heading into the cabin in time to hear Barclay say, "Baby, don't worry about the wedding. I told you, nothing is going to change. I promise, it's you and me forever."

Laramie's fists were up before he realized it.

This was what Sammi Jo was rejecting him for? This stupid, cheating jerk?

God. It was like being kicked in the head with an ugly case of déjà vu. Laramie leaned against the wall, staring out at the night-darkened bushes as memories washed over him. Another mountain, another cabin and another man with a woman he didn't deserve.

He could do it again and he'd be in the right.

Bringing that dumbass back to Sammi Jo was as good as consigning her to a life of joyless boredom playing a role that minimized her awesomeness. She'd be stuck with a guy who'd never see her as the special woman she was. Who'd never appreciate her sense of humor or her quirky honesty.

Laramie hated thinking of Sammi living that life.

But it wasn't his choice to make.

Barclay was a cheating bastard; he wasn't abusive. He wasn't putting Sammi in danger. He was simply unworthy of her. And while Laramie could hate that fact, he couldn't justify using it to take Sammi away. Because he'd learned his lesson well. He couldn't save everybody. Especially when they didn't want to be saved.

Still, as he turned back into the doorway, Laramie had

to wait for the fury at watching the man who'd be Sammi Jo's husband sweet-talk another woman. It took a couple deep breaths, then before the jerk could finish his call, Laramie stepped into the cabin and waited for the other man to look his way.

Making sure his voice was loud enough to be heard through the line, Laramie greeted, "Hey there, Barclay. Your fiancée is waiting."

12

Sammi Jo stood on the porch of Barclay House, trying to unknot the emotions tangled in her belly. But they were so messy and snarled that it was all she could do to keep from turning heel and running like hell.

The air was so hot it felt as if it was pressing down on her with the weight of all her worries. It was silent up here on the top of Main Street, the view of the town below a nagging reminder of what was at stake.

This was what she wanted, she told herself, clenching her fists as if she could squeeze the turmoil into nothingness. It was hard to care about reputations when her heart was breaking, but she couldn't let things slide. She wanted out of her engagement, and she owed Mr. Barclay the courtesy of breaking it before word of her scene with Laramie hit the town.

And she owed it to Sterling to let him down easy. Theirs might not have been a love match—or a physical match of any sort—but they were friends. She didn't want to hurt him any more than she had to.

She knew he was home. Laramie had texted her early this morning that he'd dropped him at Barclay House.

She'd waited all day to hear something more. From Sterling, or from Laramie. But neither man had contacted her.

Finally, Sammi took a deep breath. She followed that up by calling herself a yellow-bellied chicken-fueled wimp; she managed to lift the heavy brass knocker and let it fall.

Thankfully, it was opened right away, giving her less time to give in to the still nagging urge to run.

"Sammi Jo." Brows beetled together over surprised eyes, Mr. Barclay inclined his head. Dressed for a casual evening at home, he'd loosened his tie and wore a sweater instead of his suit jacket. "What are you doing here?"

"I wanted to talk with Sterling." The words came out a hoarse croak. Sammi cleared her throat and tried again. "Is Sterling available? I'd like to speak with him."

He looked as if he was debating whether or not to let her in. That's when Sammi realized she'd never actually been inside of Barclay House. For a second, she didn't think she'd make it now, either. A bubble of hysterical laughter lodged in her throat as she imagined her boss and supposed future father-in-law bellowing for Sterling to come to the door while refusing her entry. Or worse, sent her around the servants' entrance.

But after a considering look, he stepped aside to let Sammi into the glossy foyer. She wiped her feet on the welcome mat, but as she crossed the threshold she wondered if she should have removed her shoes altogether in case they marred the glass-like surface of the hardwood floors.

Curiosity outweighing nerves, she looked around. Gilt mirrors ringed the midnight-blue walls. The staircase was almost wide enough for Sammi to lie across, with two doors on either side. Her entire apartment could fit in this foyer alone.

Was her mouth hanging open?

"What a lovely…" Sammi's words trailed off as someone stepped through one of the doors on the right. No question about it, her mouth did drop open this time. Her shoulders stiffening, she closed it with a snap. "Mrs. Ross. What a surprise to see you here."

Today's jumpsuit was the same pink as that stomach medicine and just as nauseating. Instead of her usual bun, the older woman wore a braid atop her head like a crown.

"Robert and I were chatting."

Robert?

Sammi frowned at Mr. Barclay. She'd known the man for over a decade, but the only reason she knew that was his first name was because it was on her paycheck.

Suddenly it wasn't the hot pink making her ill. It was the look of triumph creasing the woman's face. Well. Sammi took a deep breath. That explained the crown.

"Mrs. Ross and I are discussing weddings at the Inn," he said comfortably, crossing the foyer to stand at the woman's side. "After careful consideration of her suggestions, I've decided that she'll run the entirety of the wedding program. And all other events, of course."

The room did a long, slow twirl as black dots danced in front of Sammi's eyes. It wasn't until the aching in her chest told her to that she realized she needed to breathe.

But offering weddings had been her idea. She'd researched for a year before proposing the project. She'd done all of the legwork, she'd done all of the groundwork. Weddings at the Barclay Inn had been her guarantee to get promoted to manager.

She wet her lips, but had to wait until the ringing cleared in her ears to speak.

"What other events?"

"Sharon believes that we're the perfect destination for a variety of events. Reunions, conventions, holiday parties." He gave Sammi what was probably supposed to be a reassuring look. "But don't worry. You'll still assist in managing the inn."

Assist.

Sammi looked at the man she'd always considered her benefactor. She'd worried so much about gossip—to the extent that she'd hurt Laramie's feelings—because of loyalty to the Barclays. But now she realized that when it came to these men, loyalty only went one way.

"Is this your final decision?" she asked quietly.

"Of course," he said assuredly. There was absolutely no discomfort or regret on his face. Was he oblivious or did he simply not care?

Feeling that heady sense of freedom calling again, Sammi decided it really didn't matter.

"Okay." She nodded. "Then if you'd be so kind, I'd like a meeting first thing Monday morning. Right now, I need to speak with Sterling."

Ignoring the other woman's smirk—and pretty much her entire puke-pink existence—Sammi followed Mr. Barclay's gesture toward the second door on the left.

Her deep breath before opening the sitting room door had nothing to do with nerves this time.

It was that delicious taste of freedom right there within her grasp. All she had to do was decide if she was going to grab it or just let it pass on by.

Pretty sure she knew the answer, Sammi strode into the sitting room, noting the sumptuous decor. Gilt and velvet seemed at odds with the uptight elder Barclay. Yet more proof that she didn't know the man.

Then she saw Sterling, looking no worse for wear as he frowned at the computer tablet he was reading.

"Hey, Sammi." Despite the lack of bushy eyebrows, his frown looked remarkably like his father's. "What are you doing here?"

And just like that, all of her worries about hurting his feelings and every vestige of loyalty to his reputation disappeared.

Sammi crossed the thick Persian rug, anger giving snap to every step. She stopped just short of Sterling's leather chair, folding her fingers into her palms to keep from smacking the man.

"Laramie sent word that he'd brought you home. Since I'd had no contact from you after your last all-is-well-in-kidnapping-land phone call, I wanted to see for myself."

Texted word, actually. Dropped your fiancé at Barclay House. Have a good life. Just thinking about it made Sammi want to cry. She hadn't thought it was possible, but she'd hurt him. And for what? Her own insecurities and a couple of men who didn't give a damn about her.

As if sensing her mounting irritation, Sterling grimaced. Setting his computer tablet aside, he rose and gave her a perfunctory kiss on the cheek.

"Sorry about that. I had a lot of damage control to handle and wanted to jump right on it." He shot a look at the doorway, then gave her a rueful smile. "And I've been stuck here listening to lecture after lecture on everything from proper business practices to the correct wording for my wedding speech."

She could only stare.

He really thought they were still getting married.

"Sterling, we need to talk."

HAD HE EVER hated the outcome of a mission more than he did the one Sammi Jo had saddled him with?

Laramie scowled his way through the last dozen-yard hike toward the cabin, wanting the beer to wash away the bitter taste in his mouth.

He'd done the right thing, rescuing that dumbass. Although it was pretty obvious that the guy could have easily rescued himself it he'd just got off his butt and put a little effort into it.

He'd done the right thing by not forcing Sammi Jo to choose between him and the dumbass.

Laramie kicked a rock out of his path, sending it flying into a tree. It ricocheted with a hard spray of bark, sailing into the dry grass with a bird-scaring thud.

God, doing the right thing sucked.

He crossed the clearing and stomped up the porch steps. Yanking off his mud-coated boots by the door, he tossed them aside to deal with after he packed.

He was getting the hell out of here.

Walking into the cabin was like getting hit in the heart with a fistful of memories.

He could see her standing in front of the fireplace in that damned second wedding dress of hers. Or curled up on the couch wearing nothing but his shirt and a satisfied smile.

He could smell her perfume, the delicate scent that reminded him of the mountains late at night.

He could hear her breath soft and even as she slept. Or fast and ragged when she came.

He could hear her voice, the sweet honesty of her words and the simple understanding in her tone. She saw him for who he was and knew him better than he knew himself.

And now she was out of his life.

Because he'd done the right thing.

Laramie pulled a beer from the fridge and ripped the cap off. He tilted back his head, upending the ice-cold liquid down his throat with a growl. Even as he finished the last drop he debated another. Instead, he tossed the bottle into the trash and headed for the bedroom.

He'd toss his things into his duffel, drop the truck off at Art's and get the hell out of Texas. Maybe there was an overseas deployment he could put in for. Something demanding and dangerous was just what he needed right now.

Then he stepped through the door and stopped short.

Sammi was in his bed. She lay on her side, her head propped on one hand, her hair spread like sunrise over his pillow.

And she was naked.

Well, there was a sheet tangled between those long, smooth legs, wrapping over the sweet curve of her hips to drape across the lush fullness of her breasts.

But Laramie knew naked. He'd specialized in it once upon a time.

For a moment he wondered if he were hallucinating. Except one beer did not a hallucination make.

Which meant that yes, indeed. Sammi Jo was naked in his bed.

He wanted to reach out and touch her. He wanted to pull her into his arms and kiss her. More, he wanted to strip that sheet away and lose himself in the heaven of her body.

But he couldn't.

Because he was doing the right thing.

But doing the right thing hurt. It physically hurt.

"What are you doing here?" Opting for caution over temptation, he asked the question from the doorway.

Hurt shone in Sammi's eyes for just a second before she blinked it away. Leaving what looked like scary determination.

"I realized a few things in the last day or so. Having my heart broke will do that to a girl," she said, her tentative smile and worried eyes at odds with her sensual pose.

Damn it all to hell. She'd asked him to find that dumbass, and he had. Wasn't that enough? He didn't want to listen to her feelings about the guy, too.

He called up his vast array of skills, not as a SEAL, but

as a man who'd had a lot of women and always left them satisfied with goodbye.

A friendly but distant smile.

Body language open but detached.

And his tone pleasant but just removed enough to indicate disinterest.

"Realizations and heartbreaks can keep a person busy, I suppose." He let his lips quirk toward a smile. "And you do look tempting enough for me to want to climb into that bed and hear all about it. But I've got to head out, sweetheart. I've got a plane to catch."

Self-preservation kept him from blinking at the lie, or at the hurt that flashed across her face.

"You're leaving? Now? Before we talk?"

He knew Sammi. All it'd take was keeping the wall between them and she'd give up. So Laramie made sure his apology came off like a shrug.

"Sorry. But like I told you the other night, we're pretty much done."

"Why?"

The question was, why wasn't she giving up? This was too damned hard for him to keep it up for long.

"Because ending it is the right thing to do. I was temporary," he reminded her, pretending that didn't eat at his gut. "For a good time, call. Remember?"

"That's not what it was," she protested quietly, her face melting into a frown and that bottom lip jutting out just enough to nibble on.

"Sammi Jo, you came after me for one thing. Help finding your fiancé."

"In the beginning, yes. Because you were the only one who could help me." She shifted into a sitting position, the move tightening the sheet against her breast and making Laramie wonder if she was trying to kill him. "But you know I've had feelings for you since that first day. You know I want you. What we have, Laramie, it's amazing. I don't want to lose that."

"So you're saying, what?" He gave her a narrow look. "You're getting married next week, but you want to have a little fun each year when I come to town? Or realize what a loser your fiancé was and decide to dump him? I guess Barclay's a pretty easygoing guy, he won't mind you working for him after you've ditched his son."

As if.

"Actually I ditched his son the night before last," Sammi said with a toss of her head. Her hair bounced on those bare shoulders, tempting Laramie to say screw the right thing and bury his face there. "And since I quit my job, I don't think it matters if Mr. Barclay is easygoing about it or not."

"You're not marrying Barclay?" he repeated, needing to hear it again.

"No."

"And you quit your job, so you no longer have any commitments that necessitate you living in Jerrick?"

She shook her head, a smile starting to play over her lips.

Everything inside him was dancing and screaming like a happy schoolboy. Except Laramie had never been a happy schoolboy, so he didn't quite trust it.

"What are your plans, then? Have you figured out the rest of your life?"

"What do you want me to do with it?" Her words were halfway between teasing and serious. Throw in the fluttering eyelashes and the sweet smile, and Laramie was a goner.

Stand strong, he ordered himself. He'd faced Hell Week. He'd fought terrorists. He could hold out against Sammi Jo's cuteness when their future was in the balance.

He hoped.

Calling up all of his training, Laramie took his cowboy hat off and set it on the dresser. He subtly came to attention. Shoulders back, chin high. And gave her a direct stare. "What are you going to do, Sammi Jo?"

The flirty bravado left her face, leaving her expression pale and unsure. But Laramie couldn't make this part easy for her.

He'd give her the world if he could.

But he had to hear her say she wanted it first.

"I have a decent amount of money saved up. I can't live on it for long, but it'll get me started." She stopped, taking a deep breath that damn near killed Laramie's resolve because it tipped that sheet into the danger zone. "I'm moving to California. I've talked with Lark, who wants to carry my cards in her gallery. She suggested a few more places for me to try, including a bookstore and a couple of publishing houses."

She'd talked to Lark? When? Why hadn't anyone told him? Without realizing it, Laramie shifted from attention to at ease, relaxing his shoulders and crossing his arms over his chest.

One hand tucking that sheet between her breasts, Sammi pushed the other through her hair as if she were trying to loosen her thoughts.

"Those realizations I had today? One of them was that I have a bad habit of giving up. I'm great at planning and working toward a goal, but when push comes to shove, I can't seem to step up." She wet her lips, her eyes on the sheet now instead of on him. "I didn't much like realizing that, but it's the truth. I did it with the inn, working my butt off chasing after the manager position. But each time I was blown off, I didn't push, I never let on that I was disappointed. I just tried to jump a little higher."

"Sammi—"

"No, please. Let me get it all out at once."

Hating to see her beat up on herself but figuring she must have a reason for it, Laramie gestured that she go ahead.

"I did the same with my art. I am good. I studied business and marketing in college with the thought in the back of my mind that I'd manage the inn to pay Mr. Barclay back, but that I'd do my art on the side so when I was ready, I could shift to art full-time. But a few setbacks, a few derogatory comments, and I set it aside. I didn't push, I didn't question that those comments were true. I simply gave up."

"And now?"

"And now, you." She met his gaze again, hers direct and strong. "I would have let you push me away. It was the easier route, after all. Oh, I wasn't going to marry Sterling. Not after his little dramafest. But I'd have let you go, because it seemed like what you wanted. But I'm done with taking the easy route."

"Are you, now?" Laramie's smile was slow, wide and heading toward satisfied.

"Yes, I am. I'm moving to San Diego. I'm not looking for a handout or for you to support me or anything. I've already called in a few favors and have a couple of interviews lined up." She took a deep breath. "Because even though you took it back, I'm taking you up on that invitation. I'm coming with you."

It was all he could do to keep his grin at bay.

"What exactly is it that you want, Sammi Jo?"

"I want you."

"Why?" And there it was. The last wall he was putting between them. Even as he set it in place, a part of him didn't expect her to give up.

"Why?" She gave him an adorable scowl. "Why else. Because I love you."

Damn. She really did love him. Other than his mother, he'd never had anyone love him enough to fight for him—not even through his own walls.

Pleasure surged, joy flared. All of a sudden, Laramie felt incredible.

His eyes locked on Sammi's, he unsnapped his shirt and shrugged it off.

"What are you doing?" Her words were somewhere between confused at his stripping and frustrated that he hadn't responded to her declaration.

"What does it look like?" He arched his brow and unbuckled his belt. "I'm giving you what you want."

Hurt flashed in her eyes, quickly replaced by appreciation as he shucked his pants. Sammi shifted from the center of the bed to one side, patting the mattress next to her. Tossing the rest of his clothes aside, Laramie joined her.

Then, because he figured he'd been teased enough, he whipped the sheet out from between them and sent it sailing across the room.

"It was in the way," he explained when she gave a gasping laugh.

Her laughter settled into a warm smile as Sammi lay back against the pillow and held out her arms. She was a dream come true. A dream he hadn't even realized he was hiding deep in his heart. His gaze moved over her lush curves, the sight of those pouting coral nipples flipping him from burgeoning hardness to freaking concrete. His fingers itched to touch. His mouth watered for the taste of her. Even his dick was getting in on the demands, needing to plunge into those dewy, soft russet curls between her thighs and find release.

But Laramie had to settle a few other things first.

"You forgot to ask me what I wanted," he said, his mouth hovering over hers. Close enough to tempt but not quite to touch.

"What do you want?" She punctuated the question by reaching between their bodies to trail her fingers in a teasing pattern down his belly.

"You." He shifted back just a little so she could see how serious he was. "I want you with me in California. I want you with me wherever I'm deployed. I want to get a place off base and build a life together."

He took her eyes widening with delight as a good sign, so continued.

"I want to show you the beach and swim in the oceans together. I want to take you around the world, to experience it all by your side." This time he was the one to take a deep breath. Then he powered through. "I love you, Sammi Jo."

He'd never said that to a woman other than his mom. So he didn't know how to take Sammi's gasp. A seed of worry danced down his spine. He wanted to believe the tears trickling down her face were a good thing, but for all his expertise with women, he wasn't sure.

"I love you, too," she said with a watery laugh. "I'll follow you anywhere."

Her words sent a shaft of emotion through Laramie so strong, so hard, that he had to close his eyes against the intensity. Needing to mitigate that power, he forced himself to give her an easy look.

"In the spirit of full disclosure, I could get assigned to some really lousy posts. I don't expect you to follow along. I want you to find where you're happiest and settle there."

"Christian, I love you." She pressed her hands against his cheeks, holding his face while she stared into his eyes. The intimacy of her look was even more powerful than her words. "And I will follow you wherever I am allowed.

If that means California or Virginia or Kandahar, I'll be there. You asked me what I want."

He nodded because he was too stunned for words.

"I want to live my life with you. I want to spend as much of it by your side as I can. I want to make a home for you that will always be waiting. A home that's easy to pack up and move." She gave him a smile brimming with joy and excitement. "I've lived my entire life in one place. I think it'd be fun to see how many places we can spend the rest of it."

Everything. He'd stepped back, unwilling to force her to choose. And she'd stepped forward, to give him everything. She was giving him the dreams he'd been afraid of dreaming.

"I'll make you happy," he promised, finally letting himself touch her, his fingers whisper soft as they trailed over her cheek.

"We'll make each other happy," she promised.

"Forever." His mouth brushed hers, echoing the promise. "We've got forever together."

* * * * *

COMING NEXT MONTH FROM

HARLEQUIN *Blaze*

Available June 21, 2016

#899 COWBOY AFTER DARK
Thunder Mountain Brotherhood
by Vicki Lewis Thompson

Liam Magee is at the ranch for a wedding—so is Hope Caldwell, whom he's wanted in his bed for months. Hope craves the sexy cowboy but can she trust him for more than a fling?

#900 MAKE MINE A MARINE
Uniformly Hot!
by Candace Havens

Having recently returned home, Marine Matt Ryan is looking forward to a more peaceful life as a helicopter instructor at the local base...not realizing free-spirited Chelly Richardson is about to rock his world!

#901 THE MIGHTY QUINNS: THOM
The Mighty Quinns
by Kate Hoffmann

Hockey player Thom Quinn has never hesitated to seduce a beautiful woman. But the bad boy has to be good this time, because Malin Pederson controls his fate on the team. And she's the boss's daughter.

#902 NO SURRENDER
by Sara Arden

Fiery Kentucky Lee burns hot enough to warm Special Ops Aviation pilot Sean Dryden's frozen heart—not to mention his bed—but he must NOT fall for his ex-fiancée's best friend...

REQUEST YOUR FREE BOOKS!
2 FREE NOVELS PLUS 2 FREE GIFTS!

HARLEQUIN®

Blaze

red-hot reads!

SPECIAL EXCERPT FROM
⊞HARLEQUIN® *Blaze*

*Liam Magee is at the ranch for a wedding—so is
Hope Caldwell, who he's wanted in his bed for months.
Hope craves the sexy cowboy, but can she trust him
for more than a fling?*

Read on for a sneak preview of
COWBOY AFTER DARK, *the second story of 2016 in
Vicki Lewis Thompson's sexy cowboy saga*
THUNDER MOUNTAIN BROTHERHOOD.

Hope was a puzzle, and he didn't have all the pieces
yet. Something didn't fit the picture she was presenting
to everyone, but he'd figure out the mystery eventually.
Right now they had a soft blanket waiting. He lifted her
down and led her over to it.

He'd ground-tied both Navarre and Isabeau, who were
old and extremely mellow. The horses weren't going
anywhere. Hope sat on the blanket like a person about
to have a picnic, except they hadn't brought anything to
eat or drink.

Liam decided to set the tone. After relaxing beside
her, he took off his Stetson and stretched out on his back.
"You can see the stars a lot better if you lie back."

To his surprise, she laughed. "Is that a maneuver?"

"A maneuver?"

"You know, a move."

"Oh. I guess it's a move, now that you mention it." He
sighed. "The truth is, I want to kiss you, and it'll be easier
if you're down here instead of up there."

"So it has nothing to do with looking at the stars."

"It has everything to do with looking at the stars! First you lie on your back and appreciate how beautiful they are, and then I get to kiss you underneath their brilliant light. It all goes together."

"You sound cranky."

"That's because nobody has ever made me break it down."

"I see." She flopped down onto the blanket. "Beautiful stars. Now kiss me."

"You just completely destroyed the mood."

"Are you sure?" She rolled to her side and reached over to run a finger down his tense jaw. "Last time I checked, we still had a canopy of stars arching over us."

"A canopy of stars." He turned to face her and propped his head on his hand. "Did you write that?"

"None of your beeswax."

Although she'd said it in a teasing way, he got the message. No more questions about her late great writing career. "Let's start over. How about if you lie back and look up at the stars?"

"I did that already, and you didn't pick up your cue."

"Try it again."

She sighed and rolled to her back. "Beautiful stars. Now kiss—"

His mouth covered hers before she could finish.

Don't miss COWBOY AFTER DARK
by Vicki Lewis Thompson.
Available in July 2016 wherever
Harlequin® Blaze® books and ebooks are sold.

www.Harlequin.com

HBEXP0616

Reading Has Its Rewards

Earn **FREE BOOKS!**

Register at **Harlequin My Rewards** and submit your Harlequin purchases from wherever you shop to earn points for free books and other exclusive rewards.

Plus submit your purchases from now till May 30th for a chance to win a $500 Visa Card*.

Visit **HarlequinMyRewards.com** today

MYR16R1

Whatever You're Into… Passionate Reads

Looking for more passionate reads from Harlequin®?
Fear not! Harlequin® Presents, Harlequin® Desire and
Harlequin® Blaze offer you irresistible romance stories
featuring powerful heroes.

♦HARLEQUIN *Presents.*

Do you want alpha males, decadent glamour and jet-set
lifestyles? Step into the sensational, sophisticated world of
Harlequin® Presents, where sinfully tempting heroes ignite a
fierce and wickedly irresistible passion!

♦HARLEQUIN *Desire*

Harlequin® Desire novels are powerful, passionate and
provocative contemporary romances set against a backdrop of
wealth, privilege and sweeping family saga. Alpha heroes with
a soft side meet strong-willed but vulnerable heroines amid a
dramatic world of divided loyalties, high-stakes conflict and
intense emotion.

♦HARLEQUIN *Blaze*

Harlequin® Blaze stories sizzle with strong heroines and
irresistible heroes playing the game of modern love and lust.
They're fun, sexy and always steamy.

Be sure to check out our full selection of books
within each series every month!

www.Harlequin.com

HPASSION2016

HARLEQUIN®

A *Romance* FOR EVERY MOOD™

JUST CAN'T GET ENOUGH?

Join our social communities
and talk to us online.

You will have access to the latest
news on upcoming titles and special
promotions, but most importantly,
you can talk to other fans about your
favorite Harlequin reads.

Harlequin.com/Community

Facebook.com/HarlequinBooks

Twitter.com/HarlequinBooks

Pinterest.com/HarlequinBooks

HSOCIAL

Dear Reader,

I knew I was going to write Christian Laramie's story from the first time he showed up on the pages of a *A SEAL's Temptation*. Not only was he a yummy SEAL with the call sign "Cowboy," but he had this way with women that made him a legend. The better I got to know him in the writing of *A SEAL's Touch*, the more one particular scene gelled in my mind. The one I knew I'd have to write his story around.

This gorgeous, lady-loving, freewheeling cowboy coming face-to-face with a runaway bride in search of a hero to rescue her groom. Sammi Jo and Laramie are so different, yet so much alike, and I truly enjoyed watching them explore those similarities and differences.

That, combined with the reunion of childhood friends, the excitement and fun of the weeks leading up to a wedding, and the bride's cold feet all came together into a story that I hope will make you smile, laugh and sigh.

I hope that you'll check out the rest of my sexy SEAL series. You can find them on my website, as well as insider peeks into this story and others. Visit tawnyweber.com or find me on Facebook at Facebook.com/tawnyweber.romanceauthor.

Happy reading,

Tawny Weber

**"Do you think I'm going to have sex with you,"
Sammi Jo murmured, "in return for you helping
me find Sterling?"**

"You're kidding, right?" Laramie said, his eyes filled
with laughter. "Sugar, I'm a highly skilled military
machine. My training alone is worth more money
than this entire town. You think you can pay me off
with a kiss?"

Well, she'd actually thought the payment would be
a lot more than just kissing.

"I don't barter with sex. I don't have to." He waited
a beat as the heat worked its way up Sammi's
cheeks. "But when we do have sex, you're going to
be the one asking."

Her mouth dropped.

She wanted to laugh. To say that'd never happen.
But as her stomach pitched into her toes, tingling
the entire way, it assured Sammi that she should be
careful.

Otherwise she was going to be in big trouble.

Big, naked trouble.

"I came here for your help," she said shakily, the
words as much for her as for him. "I'm not here to
sample your legendary sexual skills..."